SCOTT TOO

SCOTT TOO
First Edition

Copyright © 2012 by Victor Giannini
All rights reserved

This book is a work of fiction. All characters and events portrayed in it are fictitious, except where specific historical events are mentioned or cited in context. Any resemblance to real people or events is coincidental.

Printed in the United States of America

Published by Silverthought Press
www.silverthought.com

Cover art copyright © 2012 by Scott Meyers

ISBN: 978-0-9841738-9-1

SCOTT TOO

— a novella by —
Victor Giannini

[silverthought]
PHILADELPHIA | NEW YORK

Dedicated To:

Mom and Dad

Also…

This book is dedicated to you.
Yes, YOU.

Special Thanks:

K. Jones
J. Feiffer
M. Miranda
P. Hughes
R. Rosenblatt
S. Meyers
S. Snyder

And especially…

The Stony Brook Southampton
MFA in Creative Writing and Literature

The last normal day of my life began as all the others did. I woke at 7 PM, cracked my neck, and slumped downstairs to find my roommate, Jase, laid out in his corner chair. Half a burnt-out joint stuck to his dried lips, fluttering through his snores. Empty beer cans stood post around his feet, and one, half drunk, tilted over between his legs and dribbled down the cushions. I was unsure if the stain across his jeans was the beer, or if he'd pissed himself again. The constant gym sock odor of our living room made it impossible to tell. I pulled the joint away from his beard, lit it, and took a few hits.

A grocery list lay on the coffee table, pinned under a cigarette tray, itself under a volcano of burnt out butts. Jase couldn't pick them up due to his busy schedule of tattooing underage girls and getting baked all day. No matter, it was a good excuse to go to the bodega down the block and see Trish. I played some videogames and headed out at 12 AM, the start of a crisp, dark, new day.

Trish rang up my items, her short brown hair with one green streak falling over her green eyes as she estimated the prices silently. The place was tiny and empty as always around this time of night. The only other guy there was a Hell's Angels reject, smelled like a dumpster rat. Trish rolled her eyes and calculated what might be the cost of soy milk, a pack of cigarettes, a dozen eggs, a case of beer, eco-friendly laundry detergent, and a pack of magnum sized condoms.

Truth be told, only one magnum would ever leave the pack, replacing the older one in my wallet. The rest of its brothers would join the pile under my bed, a veritable army of soldiers too big for the task and ready for a war that wasn't gonna happen.

"That's uh… twenty bucks or something," Trish said.

"Okay, yeah. Twenty, cool." I fished around my pockets for bills and change. Wallet must have been in my other pants. "So um, Trish, do you…"

"How do you know my name? Do I know you?"

"We met at the Korova Bar. Like, um, a couple weeks ago? Do you…"

"Jesus Christ, man, just pay her and get out," the fat man said. His leather jacket creaked as he shifted around with a case of booze under each armpit. "Seriously, bro. You're pissing me off. Finish up with her and get on with your life."

That's when it happened.

All sound became pops and explosions, glass shattering and spraying inward, cigarettes and horny goat weed, bottles, gum, and chocolate bars showering the three of us. We moved in unison, ducking forward, arms around our heads, all making the same shriek. Something hot slid past my left eye, tires squealed, tiny pops echoed down the street in response, and we three fell into a pit of silence. Trish looked up, still hunched. We locked eyes.

"Are you alright?" we asked in unison. "What?" we did it again. "I can't hear you!"

The silence faded into a loud ringing. Eardrum cells calling out in pain. I stood up, touching the side of my head, then peered out the shattered window behind Trish. No one on the streets. Just purple concrete bathed in yellow lamplight.

"You're bleeding."

I touched the left side of my head. It was hot and wet, but my vision was fine and the ringing was fading. I stepped back, hit a solid pillow, and tumbled back into a pile of wheat bran flakes, cold baked beans, milk, and shattered glass. Trish gasped.

I looked at my legs, not draped over a pillow, but over the dead Hell's Angel. Propped up on my shoulders, finding the sludge of cheap food on my back and hair more unnerving than his blood soaking into my argyle socks.

"What the hell was that?" I asked. "Did we just get hit by a drive by?"

"Yeah, dude. That was definitely a drive by," she said, staring behind her to make sure the street was still dead empty. She folded her arms across her breasts, but her eyes were stretched wide.

"Um, it's Scott."

"What?"

"My name is Scott. Dude is my last name."

Trish stared at me. I expected her to laugh and get the joke, forgetting that a dead man's blood was slowly seeping below my ass.

"You guys don't have an alarm here?"

She shot me a *no shit* look.

"We have to call the police," she said. She walked over to help me up, reached out, and then reflexively stepped back as her soles felt the sticky red mess. She tracked blood around behind the counter, looking for the phone. My hand stayed frozen, fingertips singing in pain at how close they'd come to actual physical contact. "Dude, are you okay?"

"Why?" I touched the side of my eye again. "Oh, no, I'm fine. Could you just uh… could you bag those up for me?"

"Are you serious?"

"Oh. Ha, no way. No, I'm not serious. Don't worry, yeah, I got it." I got up, reached behind the counter for a green plastic bag, and stuffed my stuff in it. I put the pack of magnum condoms in very slowly, hoping the black and gold box would catch Trish's eye. Very slowly.

She put the phone down. "They're gonna be here in ten minutes."

"The precinct's like... three blocks away," I said.

She shrugged.

"You know," I said, breathing in and gritting my teeth. "I think I'm gonna go... I don't really like... cops."

"Yeah, yeah, I feel you." Trish was staring around, shaking her head and running her hands through her hair. She still hadn't blinked.

"I'll be back though."

"What? Why?"

"To see if you're okay."

"I'm... I'm fine, I just gotta... Shit, I gotta get a new job now."

The dead man groaned. We both glanced back at him.

"Oh shit, he's alive!" Trish said. "They'll bring an ambulance, right? Should I call back? Shit. You sure you don't want them to look at your face?"

"Why, is it messed up?"

"Your eye is kinda red and puffy—I think you got grazed. But other than that..."

"I'm fine?" I patted myself down, chest, thighs, arms, and legs. Lots of high fructose juices, but no pain.

"Yeah, you're fine."

"Not as fine as you," I said, smiling and cocking my fingers at her like guns, click click. Yeah.

"Look, I get it, you're trying to be funny, but I'm a little shook up."

"Sorry. Look, I live down the street. I have a sweet apartment if you need a place to um... wind down. Maybe talk about what happened?"

"What? No thanks. I have my own place, dude."

"Scott."

"Right, Scott."

"Can you do me a favor? Don't tell the cops I was here or anything. It's not like I can really help and I'm not so fond of pigs."

"Sure dude, whatever."

"Okay. Later, Trish. Glad we didn't get shot!" I pushed against the bodega door but felt night air. My hand went right through a jagged hole. I pulled it back in so as not to slice my wrist. I gently kicked the door open and stepped out into that strange New York night air, both cool and heavy at the same time. I peeked in every direction. Still no one in sight. Light pollution taking center stage. The pigeons were already returning. I looked back through the window, but Trish was gone. I lit one of Jase's cigarettes. The brief flame made my eye burn.

And then it hit me.

I didn't get hit.

That place went up like it was rigged with M-80s. The guy behind me got hit. Sure, he was twice as big a target, but still. Not even my groceries got shot. I must have had a million bullets whiz right by me, and not a single one connected. At times like this you gotta ask yourself, why? Why not me? Why did the guy behind me get tagged and I just froze like a dumbass and didn't even get hit in the leg or nothing? By all logic I... I should be dead.

So why am I alive?

Trish didn't get hit either, and she was closer to the street than I was. Maybe we're blessed. It's fate! We're destined to survive and have a happy family. Or at least lots of sex. That would be a good start. And it all starts with her just... remembering my freaking name.

Walking into the tunnel under the BQE, I shifted the bag and case of beer around, rubbing my face to make sure I really was fine. By the time I was down the block, walled in by brownstones and iron-gate fences, I felt my adrenaline fading, but the question persisted.

Why that guy? Why not me? I should have felt grateful. I won the lotto and the prize was life. But... what kind of life? I'm nearly thirty, work for a porno company, and my roommate is a pot dealer and tattoo artist. I haven't had a date in three years. I used to have a life I was proud of and now it's like I just woke up from a very long, very boring dream. I know what happens next. I'll get home, get wasted with Jase, watch TV, work at my computer for Sohotforteacher.com or something, rinse and repeat. And Trish might not even be at the bodega tomorrow.

Shit! I was about to turn back but was frozen by the echo of sirens. So I shuffled back down the block, hopped down the steps to our entrance, pulled the black grate back and pushed the door open to reality. I stepped into the living room and saw Jase in the same chair, awake, and... talking to me on the couch.

"Yo, Scott!" Jase said. "You didn't tell me you had a twin."

I stared at myself staring back at me. My cigarette fell.

"Jase... I don't have a twin."

I clutched the grocery bag to my chest. There was no mistaking it. Same shaggy black hair, same bony thin face, same three moles on the right side of the head, even the same plaid overcoat and ripped jeans I was wearing right then.

"Hi," he said.

"What the fuck kind of joke is this? Look, I just went through some crazy shit... I can't take this right now. Whatever joke you guys are playing, I'm not in the mood."

Jase got up and took the case of beer from me, then immediately returned to his sofa chair under the shade-less lamp.

"Man, I must be really high," he said. He leaned on his elbow, the crack of a fresh beer echoing among the three of us.

I thumbed behind me. "Look, I was just in a drive by and I almost died. I'm really um... in shock I guess. Seriously, I almost got killed. Look at my face!"

"Well, I did die," the other me said.

"Is that chick okay?" Jase asked, leaning back.

Couch imposter was staring at me, complacent.

Still standing in the door, feet cemented to the carpet, the shaking came. It rose from the arches of my feet, up my shinbones, through my pelvis, spine, ribcage, and exploded dead center in my head. My eye finally burned in full force.

"Who the hell are you? How did you get in here? Jase, how did this guy get in here?"

"I dunno, man. I went upstairs to take a piss, and when I came back down you were just sitting on the couch."

"That's not me!"

"Yes I am," the other me said, cool as hell.

"What's your fucking name then?"

"Scott Alvin," he said.

"No, my name is Scott Alvin! Jase, don't you find this a little fucking strange?"

"Hell yeah I do," he said. Jase lit a blunt, puffed a few times, and looked up at us. He squinted and pursed his lips. He spoke directly to me. "Hey, if you're both you, then how do I know you're not the fake you? What proof you got you're the real Scott?"

What? Was he serious? Jase copes like no one else, but this is just... just... I felt the plastic green bag crinkling under my armpit. I hugged it tighter.

"I'm holding the goddamn groceries you sent me for!"

"That's a good point," other me said. He spread his arms across the back of the couch. "He must be him."

"Aight," Jase said. Satisfied, he took a few more hits, clouded the room with his skunky exhale, and then passed the blunt to the guy on the couch. "Well relax, man. Have a hit and put the bag down."

No way was I putting the bag down. It was my only proof. I took Jase's cigarettes out of the bag and threw them at his head. He laughed as the pack hit the stinky cushion.

"What happened to your eye?" he asked.

"Look, I'm seriously not concerned about my fucking eye right now!"

"Hey, chill out. You didn't get shot in the face five minutes ago! I got killed. I'm a little shook up," the couch monster said. He crossed his lanky arms and scowled.

"Then why do you look perfectly okay?" I asked.

He touched his face, chin, and eye sockets, rubbed around to the back of his head. "I don't know why I look okay. But I do know that I was shot, and killed, and now I'm back here."

"Well, I know something," Jase said. We turned to him. "I'm going to pack this giant bong here with some killer weed. And we're only going to smoke it and chill out, and then we'll eat some nachos, and then we'll figure out where exactly reality broke apart. Aight?"

He reached around for his bong, pulled out a big bag of purple crystal encrusted weed, and jammed it full. He looked up at me, and then used his head to point at the couch. "Sit down."

I approached the couch slowly, my eyes locked with my own eyes, and sat down at the very edge of the couch, closer to Jase. Every crinkle of the bag against my chest, the rumple of the cushions under my weight, the crunchy crackle of the weed packing, everything, sounded like the scream of giant insects in an empty cave.

"Wait!" Jase shouted.

My heart was right about at its freak out limit. "What? What the hell is it now?"

"Maybe you guys shouldn't touch," Jase said. He looked honestly concerned. "You know, like, what if you blow up reality?"

"What are you… Jase, do you really think the universe is going to cease to exist if I touch myself?" I asked.

"If that were true, we'd be doomed every time Jase locked his door," other me said.

I laughed, turned, and gave him a high five. But we stopped mid-air, the space between our hands charged with the unknown… then both pulled our hands away slowly. For a moment, I thought I wasn't so bad after all. My hold on the bag relaxed.

"I read some shit once, talked about how two things can't exist in the same place at the same time," Jase said as he rolled up the last of his weed and stuck it inside his jacket. "It's a contradiction or something."

"Are you sure you read that?" I asked Jase. "Wasn't that how that shitty movie 'Time Inspector' ended? You don't have the biggest book collec—"

"I think that has to do with time travel theory," the other me spoke over my shoulder. "Quantum mechanics and reality hyper strings or something."

Jase passed me the bong. Of course, I knew what I meant. I mean, the other me.

"You know what, you're worried about reality breaking down? I think we're already there, guys," I said.

Fuck it.

I put the bong on the glass coffee table, turned around, and gave myself a hug. I clenched my teeth, shut my eyes, and waited for the universe to implode.

After one strangely normal hug (I never realized I was so bony), and a round of lung splitting bong hits, we were still alive, and my dead clone was still there. The universe had not eaten itself alive. But the weed was eating my senses away slowly, making everything just that much easier to deal with. My head tilted and swirled, all the words coming up like bubbles rising in a pool. In this space of an hour, everything was the same as I'd left it, and yet would never be the same again.

Same small living room, an archway opposite our front door leading to a rectangular, cheese encrusted, moldy dish graveyard, with another door at the far end leading to our "back yard." Same old knobbed TV with real wood paneling, that, truth be told, we could upgrade to an HD plasma screen 1080p if we took the time to bother. Same old school videogame systems on top of milk crates against the wall, all courtesy of Jase's marijuana business, but still the same old games we played growing up. Same paisley couch, to the left of the front door. Same stained rug, same coffee table hidden under empty beer cans, skate magazines, cigarette trays, and Chinese food cartons. Same staircase to the left of the couch, leading up to my room. Same three lamps, the tall one without a cover hanging over Jase's head.

Same Jase, same leather jacket creaking apart, same slowly growing gut and don't give a shit attitude, a little out of touch, perpetual scruff and bags under his eyes. Same infectious smile, same relaxed lethargy and dirty jeans, ironic t-shirt. Same diseased throne he always sat and often slept in.

Except two of me. I turned to him.

"So you're really me, eh? What was Mom's maiden name?"

"Metzger."

"And what was Dad's middle name?"

"Thomas."

"My... our first girlfriend's name?"

"Gina."

"Last time we got laid?"

"About three years ago."

"Who? Where?"

"Alex, on the roof."

"Alex?" Jase asked.

"Alexandra," we said in unison.

"Hey, it's cool. I don't judge." Jase presented his palms and leaned back.

I looked at Jase suspiciously. Of course he knew about Gina and my dry spell, but even he didn't know the info about my parents.

It's said that the human being is one of the most adaptable species in existence. It's truly amazing what we can accept when we have to. Jase packed the bong twice and we passed some beers around, and suddenly my supernatural imposter was just another guy on the couch, a long lost relative being interviewed.

"What should we call you?" I asked.

"Scott," he said.

"No, I'm Scott." I turned to Jase for backup, being stuck between them.

"Or Scott One," other me said.

"No, I'm Scott. Just Scott. I'm the original, I'm Scott, I'm staying Scott," I said, clutching the grocery bag tighter to my chest.

"What about Scottimus Prime?" Jase said, moving his arms like a robot and making the classic cartoon Transmutators sound. The other me laughed. Of course he liked it, I liked it, and it's a fact that Trans Prime does kick ass. But I wasn't about to start referring to this thing after an '80s cartoon.

"Well, I guess you can be Scott, too," I said.

"Scott Two. Fine. Whatever, man. After catching a bullet in the skull, I really don't care what you guys call me," Scott Two said.

"What about Chuck?" Jase said. He lit three cigarettes and passed two. Scott Two and I stared at him. "What? Just a suggestion."

"Okay, now that that's out of the way," I said. "There's a lot of questions I need answered."

"Shoot."

Jase laughed. Scott Two grimaced.

"Sorry... um... Scott Two. What's the last thing you remember?"

"I was at the bodega. I was talking to Trish, and some fat asshole behind me said something, and then there was an explosion of sounds, the side of my head lit up like a firecracker, I smelled sulfur, and that was it."

"And then..."

Jase coughed. "Yeah, like, then what? God? Devil? Heaven? Hell? Was it like a Dead Corpse video?"

"Why would you assume I'd go to hell?" I asked Jase. "I'm a nice guy! Aren't I?"

"Relax. I just think it'd be cool." He shrank back and lifted his bong onto his lap.

"No, I just floated around in the dark, and I just knew, man. I just knew I was dead. It felt like the left half of my head was missing, and I felt this wet dripping, and heard this sound like... like some ancient machine clanging in the darkness, except it wasn't dark. Because dark is the absence of light, you know. This wasn't like that. It was just nothing."

"Sounds kinda scary," I said. I stared down at the carpet.

"Then I felt falling, really sick, like I was going to puke all my guts right out my mouth, and then boom, softness, everything shines and burns, and I'm back on the couch. Jase came downstairs and started talking about smoking up his new Polar Medusa strand, and then you came home."

We all chewed the information over.

"So there's no afterlife then?" I asked.

"Dude, this IS his afterlife."

Scott Two nodded.

Wow, that is really creepy.

"But look, I mean, you're wearing the same clothes as me, but your head is fine, you're not covered in the filth that I am." I stopped short. I hate being sticky more than anything. I still hadn't changed or washed my hair. I stroked the wound beside my eye. Not deep, like a bad scratch. But sticky. Can't be sticky.

"Dude, I don't fucking know," he said. "By the way, how did things go with Trish?"

"Huh?"

"Last thing I remember, we were talking about that bar…"

"Oh, I got shot down. Um, I mean we got shot down… Jeez. Poor choice of words?"

"Well, look on the bright side." Jase clapped his hands like a gunshot. "Now we can split the rent three ways!"

"How? He can't exactly go out and get a job!"

"Why not?"

Scott Two lifted his arm in the air. "I'm going to officially announce myself as in favor of me not getting a job." He leaned out across the rest of the couch, feet up on the coffee table.

"Well, I can't exactly have two of me running around the neighborhood." But then I realized… I work from my computer. I turned to Scott Two and grabbed his knee. "Hey, if we're both doing web maintenance for those porn companies, we can work for twice as many clients and make twice as much cash!"

"That's fucking rad," Jase said, holding in a burp. He lit up another joint. "Do it! Lemons out of hand grenades or something."

"Look, guys, I just died and came back to life. I'm not exactly trying to return to the daily grind."

"Well, how long you plan on sticking around?" Jase asked.

"Excuse me?" Scott Two said.

"Scott ain't the only one who's gotta deal with you. I got two roommates now, and you didn't pop back onto Earth with an extra bedroom. So pay your share or get the fuck out."

"Chill, Jase," I said. "Where am I going to go? I mean where is HE gonna go?"

"I'm not pissed, I'm saying it's awesome to have two of my best friends, but only if they're both paying rent. We don't need no freeloading couch surfer, undead or not."

"I don't think I'm undead," Scott Two said, looking down his body and poking himself in the chest. He thumbed at me. "He looks more of a mess than I do."

"Regardless, Jase has a point. If you're me, then you're going to feel guilty for not doing your share anyway."

Scott Two sighed, looked at the ceiling, glanced around the room, stretched, yawned, wiggled his shoes off onto the floor, and then shut his eyes. "Alright. Deal. So what happened with Trish? I assume she's fine, or you'd be losing your mind."

"Maybe I already have."

Jase threw an empty beer can at my head. I shrank to the side and just missed it.

"Nope, you seem just fine to me," he said.

"C'mon, I assume she's okay. You're fairly calm, all things considered," Scott Two said.

"Yeah, she's fine. It's funny, only that fat jerk got hit. I'm not sure if he died or not."

Scott Two sat up. "He got shot?" He laid back and laughed. "At least Trish is okay."

My eye began to burn again. I held a beer can against it, staring at the old plaster ceiling. "Yeah, she's okay. I'm okay. Everything's okay. Everything's okay."

"Good," Jase said. "You know, this might turn out to be pretty bad."

"Yeah... it could be pretty bad," I said.

"No, dude. Rad. I said this could turn out pretty rad."

I mustered a fake laugh. "Right. That's what I meant too."

"Man, I am hiiiiiigh," Jase said, just before he fell back into a full-bore snore.

Scott Two had passed out in the interim as well. I threw myself back against the couch, drifting into sleep, wondering if Trish had some kind of weird clone at home too.

Thank god it was all just a nightmare. Slits of sun crept through the blinds. I threw my arm over my eyes and slept past noon. I awoke far earlier than usual, around 2 PM. I cracked my neck, rubbed my sore eye, and took inventory.

I was alone, dry mouthed, still on the couch. A sticky rip from the cushion reminded me to go shower and change immediately. The hot steam cleared my lungs, the hot water cleared my mind, and all the weird thoughts of demon clones and far-out roommates evaporated on the mirror. I even shaved. Grabbed a clean pair of pants hidden under my bed, and stumbled downstairs, my ripped jeans barely clinging to my waist.

When I walked back downstairs, I suffered another minor vascular distress. Jase was back in his chair. At 3 PM. And awake. "Where the hell did you come from?"

"I was at the store," he said, shaking a large, purple can in his hand. "I hardly slept. Needed to drink this shit."

"What's wrong?"

"Scott Two is a pain in the ass."

No.

No. No. No.

"He woke up and just started ranting like... well, like you. Bastard kept me up all night, talking about quantum this and that, and ancient gods and synthetic devils and shit," Jase said, rolling his head around. He pinched his eyes. "It's like he was afraid of sleep. Fucking Energizer Bunny, man. How am I supposed to go to work like this? I have to drink this shit just to stay awake!"

He held up a purple and yellow neon striped can the size of a sawed off shotgun. It loudly proclaimed that it was "turbo-juiced malt liquor 15% alcohol with taurine, caffeine, neoprene, guarana extract, Red #40, and guaranteed to drive you loco." He tossed the empty can across against the wall.

"This stuff tastes like the flu. Seriously, bro…"

"You know, we got a lot of empty cans littering this place. It's starting to stink… Wait, where did you get that drink?"

"At the bodega, dumbass."

"It's open? You went there today?"

"Yes," he said patiently.

"Where is it?"

"Huh?"

"Jase! Where is Scott Two?"

"I don't know, man. He's not a pet. I finally managed to get some sleep and when I woke up he was gone. He's not in your room or something?'

"No. No, it's definitely not in my room."

"Then I guess he went out."

My imposter went out. Out and about in town, doing god knows what. I mean, I could imagine what… what I would do, but even last night I had a hard time reading him. He went to see Trish! I pulled my pants up. By the time my belt was buckled I was already hustling down the street.

The BQE tunnel mocked me, each step making the bodega at the end seem another step farther, the broken yellow police tape surrounding its entrance. My footsteps danced across the brick walls, echoing back into my wounded eye, pulsing sounds of concrete and rubber bouncing like pebbles on a broken eggshell. Two kids skated past, their wheels echoing off the wall.

Of course! Skateboarding!

Why walk when I could skate there in a minute? Slash some curbs, grind, pop an ollie or two… Yeah, that used to get them. Girls love skating. One of the infamous exes explained it while Jase and the crew shredded our homemade ramp some years ago. She said it was the way we moved our hips, the way we got sweaty and cut up and obsessed. Surely Trish was something like the others. Maybe if I just spent an hour or so having a good session in front of the bodega, she'd notice my hips. Except I hadn't skated in… I can't even remember. Could I even do the tricks anymore?

The stores beside the bodega were taped off, the hair salon and the magazine shop with the gambling fold-up table in the back. They had bullet holes in their windows and the bricks around, but all I could focus on was the shattered glass of the bodega window, bulging inward. My pace slowed as the bodega drew near. I stepped through the broken police tape. Into our cigarettes, beer, bacon, and soda shrine. I held my breath. No one inside besides the owner, his pure white hair hanging elegantly over his dark brown skin as if no bullets had pierced his walls. I peered around the diaper aisle, around the dry goods and canned specialties with my back reflected across coffins of chocolate, pecan nut, vanilla, and pistachio. No Scott Two.

No Trish.

"Um, excuse me…"

"Yes, yes, we stay open. No big deal. Fucking gangsters! Who were they shooting at anyway? Degenerates."

"Is Trish coming in today?"

"Trish?"

"Yeah, white chick with green eyes. Green streak in her hair."

"No, she's not coming back in. She works very cheap and keeps up well, but now we have to cut back because of the damage. And she doesn't feel safe anyway."

"She quit? That's it? She's just gone? Do you know where she went?"

"Sir, she came in here with you," he said. His eyes were heavy, scanning me. "Remember? She left here with you this morning. She quit right in front of you."

Oh no…

"Right. I left with her… but she went home first. We were supposed to meet up, I guess I kinda forgot." I stared at the counter, rubbing my hand through my greasy hair and faking a laugh.

"You left here with her. Call her or something. It's not my business."

I thought of my outdated cell phone in my room with the old locked trunk. Did it even still work?

"Can I use your phone?"

"No."

"Okay, great, glad you're still open!" I said too quickly. "I buy everything from here. All the time, I come here every night! But really, I forgot where I was going to meet her. Do you remember what we talked about?"

"Listen, Trishandra Marquis quit today. Are you going to buy anything?"

Blind panic, scanning the aisles. A hot dog platform with wrinkled flesh rotating in the heat. Racks of juices, alcoholic and not.

"Gimme a pack of Camels and tell me where—"

"A pack of Camels, yes. Fifteen dollars."

"Fifteen! Look, fine, just tell me… remind me where I'm supposed to meet—"

"Trishandra's life is her life. I have no concern for her personal plans unless they affect the store. And now they don't. She's gone."

"Fuck the Camels." I stormed out.

"Sir, wait, I—"

The sun, so hot, so bitter and silent. Had to cover my left eye. I was home in record time. Turned the key, kicked the door open, fell into the cool darkness of the living room. Jase was comatose in the corner.

"Where the fuck is it?"

He jerked from sleep. Dead cigarettes and empty beers shed from him like bird feathers.

"It? Oh shit, Scott, what time is it? I was supposed to be at the shop at three!"

"It's almost four. Where is Scott Two? Answer me, Jase! He's been missing all day and he's out there somewhere with her and who knows what he's doing to her!"

"Doing to her?" Jase got up and pulled his leather jacket around him, tussled his pants into place, stroked his hair back. "Dude, if he's you, what would you be doing to her? Huh? Making an ass of yourself. I can't believe she even went with you."

"She went with it!" I swung my hand back toward the door.

"Whatever, same difference. I gotta go. Seriously, I need money, like yesterday. You do too, man. Rent's coming up."

"Jase!"

"Sorry, bro."

The door shut.

The damp room gave refuge, the light filtered so finely you can see the bubbles floating around you, the smell of hidden pizza and man sweat. Sweat sock tomb. Alone. The lack of footsteps. Of TV. Of cockroaches clicking in the walls. No cushions shifting, or music pumping through tenement walls...

Jase is gone.

Scott Two is real.

And he's out there with my girl. And I'm left alone, two days behind work, and rent breathing down my neck. I fell onto the couch.

I found one of Jase's half killed joints, sleeping in the ashtray with its more cancerous cousins.

Lit it. Took a deep breath. Fell back against the couch, my laptop upstairs begging to give me money if I could just get up and get back to work.

Fuck it. Fuck the porn sites, fuck the rent, fuck Jase, fuck Trish, and fuck me.

Fuck me, I gotta pay rent.

With Jase and Scott Two on their own quests and me with no leads, it came time to do something, and that something was make money. There never was a light for our staircase, yet I nearly banged my head on the overhang as I passed the bathroom towards my room. I closed the blinds, unused to working in sunlit hours. All the posters on the wall, cyberdemons, Zeno's paradox, hell chicks from Mars, and old punk bands with their spikes and snarls, all these fantastic escapes, faded into blue hues. My dad's old trunk at the base of my bed, the army of highly detailed limited edition action figures watching... my private royal tomb.

And the photographs on the wall beside my giant bed... the small gallery of girls who'd stolen my heart, yet left me feeling like I could keep playing that game. And so we all broke each other's, as if they were cars that could always be repaired.

I grabbed my laptop off the desk, careful not to knock over the week-old vegetable lo mein. I stared at the monitor on my lap, at the dirty food, ran my fingers through my hair, and then gathered up an armful of empty beer bottles. I carried the old food and drinks down to the kitchen.

God, what a hellhole. I almost gagged, wondering when I really opened my senses up to what we were living in. The sink was clogged with food-covered plates. The water brown, with little islands of whole wheat flakes, noodles, crackers, salami... Salami? Pools of melted ice cream swirled, their coloring making interesting little patterns in the sludge, little nebulas of pistachio and rocky road. They slowly dissipated around the chipped dishes, each one arching up out of the water like a sinking ship.

It's just a clogged sink. I should reach down into all the muck and pull the drain. Dig around whatever's bred down there, let it drain, and just wash them. That's all there is to it.

I stood there a while. A while longer. Decided to pour soap in instead. And of course... the dishwashing soap was ninety percent water, a clever trick when it was actually half full. I tossed everything in the trash and stomped it down with my foot. Lo mein squished up over my shoe and something wet got into the holes I didn't realize lined the sole.

I looked out the barred window to the dead skate ramp Jase and I built in our glory days, now twisted and warped and rotten. And then back to the sink.

I'll clean it tomorrow. I swear. I'll do it tomorrow.

Back in my room, I shoved everything off my bed onto the bare wood floor, kicked off my shoes, sniffed around for the cleanest pair of socks, and opened up my laptop. Time to dive back into fantasyland. I had a list of websites catering to various fetishes, all of which needed constant maintenance. It was tedious, eye searing work. In fact, the computer monitor really irritated my left eye. It felt a little swollen, dried out, just along the skin surrounding it.

So, what did I have for today? I opened up my electronic notepad: several butt play sites, a golden shower, a roman shower, latex, transgender, gangbang, amateur, hidden camera, gay, lesbian, orgies, anal, water sports... My god. How did all this become normal? When exactly did seeing fake people have fake sex, with fake enthusiasm, leave me with no more emotion than annoyance at coding, recoding, and checking the links? How did I become so numb?

This job used to be a joke. A conversation starter. Back when Jase and I tore up the city, crashed parties, boards in hand, thrashed parking lots at night with the old crew. Back when rent was frightening and every night could be our last, because we were young and dumb, but had no idea how much longer there was to go.

I flicked a roach off my pillow. Rent.

So my job: The lure is to offer just enough free content through various parent sites that people—or, rather, men with credit cards—need to pay for subscriptions to the real sites for more wanking. The companies offer a few video clips to entice, but like all desperate men, these savvy horny bastards always find a loophole in the system. Oftentimes it's simple. Scan the URL at the top of the sample screen, find which website directory was being sampled, change the number from something like 153/1.mov, to 152/2.mov, and bam! Other times I have to go into the actual html and do actual work and coding. Tedious and boring. But when I'm done, the ones who pay get a new smiling face spawned from drug use and a pair of tribal tattooed arms gripping her hips. I highly doubt there is a single person under 35 who's paid for pornography since 1998. It doesn't make sense, yet eighty-five percent of the Internet is pornography and it still turns a profit with all these slackers and moochers wasting their energy on stealing fake sex instead of landing some real action.

Most of these fetish sites are owned by the same company, working out of a huge warehouse in California (a restored WWII munitions depot, actually), which hires armies of freelancers like me to stay one step ahead of the people like me. It's a daily task, a constant game of chess that requires endless hours of monotonous...

What the fuck?

Check. Double check. My work queue is correct, but my programmed task manager says all the scheduled sites are... completed? Doesn't take a detective to realize Jase did not sneak up here and become a computer programmer overnight to clear my workload out of the kindness of his heart.

Goddamnit!

Scott Two did my job.

The bastard went ahead and cleared the day for me, did all the work, gave me time to use how I wanted... and then stole away time with Trish. But maybe he didn't steal her? Maybe he... maybe he just figured she might be quitting and went to go find out where we could find her. After all, I had the same thought last night before I... before I chickened out.

The door slammed. I went downstairs, my stomach burning.

He was standing there, arching his back and stretching. Yawning.

"Where have you been?"

"I went out for the day."

"You can't do that!"

"Why the hell not? It's not like I was out robbing banks or nothing."

"Because whatever you do out there, then I have to make sure I do something consistent when I'm out there living MY life!"

"So what, you want a checklist or something? Fine. By the way, I cleaned up the websites last night while you slept on the couch. I used the bed when I was done. Hope you don't mind."

"I uh... Well..." I sat on the couch. Head in hands, elbows on knees. "Yeah, thanks. Leaves me time to..."

"You wanna go skateboarding?"

I looked up at him in disbelief.

"No, I don't want to go skateboarding, I want to know what you did with Trish."

His lips made the same weird side to side move I do when I'm buying time.

"Hey, your eye is looking pretty bad." He approached me, reached out to touch the side of my face. "Ew, dude, did you even clean that scratch out? It looks pretty deep. And it's almost connecting with your eye socket."

I swatted his hand away. "What do you care? What did you do with Trish?"

"I chopped her up and put her in a bag. She's in the garbage outside. Jesus Christ, Scott, calm down. I'm only trying to help."

"Impersonating me and stealing my girl isn't helping!"

"Whoa, whoa, whoa. First of all, she's not your girl, at all, in any way. Second of all—"

"Right, she's your girl now, huh?"

"No! Dude, she thinks we're a total loser."

He sat down on the couch next to me. We stared at the pyramid of trash atop the coffee table.

"Are we?"

He grinned. "Well, yeah. But not for long."

Before I could react, he was bounding up the stairs to our—my—room. I took a deep breath, lit a cigarette, and cracked my neck. As I took the first step, I heard grunting coming from my room.

I peered around the corner, afraid to find me playing with myself.

He was doing pushups.

"What are you doing?"

"Pushups."

"Why?"

"Because we're scrawny and we need to start taking care of ourselves. I was asking Trish if she had a boyfriend. Something you never did, by the way. And she does. They're not too serious. He doesn't pay enough attention to her. Talks about himself a lot and he's the new bartender at the Korova, so she doesn't really trust his fidelity. But he's buff. And great in bed. I'd like to think we are, but… We ain't exactly buff, so…"

"Okay, stop. Tell me everything that happened with her today, and I'll consider not—"

"Not what? Kicking my ass? You better start doing some pushups too if you want that to happen." He was smiling up at me as he rose and fell. He wasn't angry at all.

Scott Two was happy.

I was tired, and pissed, and… scared? I sat down on the bed and watched him grunt out set after set, until his skinny arms were shaking to lift him one more time. They shook like saplings in a storm and he seemed to stall out halfway, and then with a roar, he pushed himself up completely. He rolled over onto the floor.

"Okay, so I went to the bodega as soon as she got there," he huffed. "Her shift starts at noon today, as you know. I figured she was gonna quit or get fired, and since we never really asked her anything at all, I had to do some digging so I could stay on the trail."

"We could stay on the trail," I corrected him.

"Right. You know what's funny?"

I shook my head.

"When I walked in, she smiled. Well, as close as she gets, anyway. More like one side of her lip curling up. And guess what? She said hi. This time she remembered our name."

Scott Two's late-nighter, and early morning Trish, left him beat. So I left him in my bed while I played video games downstairs. I decided to take the time to play some old-school video games and just relax. And I played better than ever! I was on a roll, despite the bad weirdness and Scott Two's vague intentions. A few beers and a few hours blasting mutants did the trick. Normally I need my partner in crime to do this well. When Jase and I join forces, we usually smash right through the bonus world. I almost did it alone today. Speak of the devil, Jase came home in the early evening, and I was already on level 20 of Death-Splitter 7, without losing a single life.

"Hey, Jase."

"What up, Scott… Two?"

"Very funny."

He collapsed into his chair. "Bro, I know it's you. That nasty eye gives it away. When you gonna get it checked out?"

"Not until I start losing vision. It's just a scratch. Besides, no insurance. You know how it is."

"Aight. It is pretty bad ass looking. But if it's just a nasty scratch and clears up, what are we gonna do? You know, for telling you guys apart?"

Good question. Even if Jase's brains finally turned to mush, I still had the problem of Scott Two sneaking off and causing trouble in my name. Or causing anything in my name. If he got outside first, I was trapped inside. I could say he was my twin. That might fly for a little while. But not in court. And he's mutating or something. He looks like me but already I feel he's not... We shared a life up until two nights ago. Now he has his own and yet he knows everything about me. But I don't know about him. He's already broken out and spent time with Trish. What if he does something stupid? Beats up an old woman or turns into a junkie? Roofies some girl while wearing my face? I mean, I would never do something like that, but he...

And Trish. I don't give a crap if I have to lie about having a twin, but he already spent more time with her in one day than I have in weeks.

The television blared, "GAME OVER! THE UNIVERSE REMAINS IN PERIL! CONTINUE?"

What the hell? I'd been stressing over Scott Two so hard that I not only lost my winning streak, I lost all my lives. Game over. And Jase was talking to me for... how long now?

"...and I was like, yo, she don't have a tattoo, but I mean look at her. This girl's body was way too slamming to be under 18. Plus, I told her it'd be two fifty for a hundred-dollar tat, and she didn't even blink."

"So she was either young and naïve, or rich and naïve. I'm in shock of your deft manipulation."

"Yeah, well, you ain't at the shop. You work in your room whenever you want, get to wank to some primo porn while getting PAID. I gotta take what I can get, and as much I as possible with the hours I get. Dude, I tattoo so fast now I could..."

I smiled. Turned off the game.

"I have an idea. I'm going to need your help. Your finest tools, and your strongest weed."

"Yeah, what we gonna do?"

"Hold on. I have to go find my handcuffs first."

Jase is an excellent partner in crime.

But before we get to that, it's time for a confession.

Despite my record breaking dry spell, I indeed have had girlfriends before. About four and a half serious ones (you know how that crap goes). The first was the high school sweetheart who broke my heart when she got to college. The second was my rebound, a cute little number with stars in her eyes and math on her mind. I realized she grew too attached too quick, and it was going to seriously break her heart when she realized I wasn't as serious. So I let her go. I like to think our breakup saved her worse pain than if I kept it going to get laid. I still like to think that. Third photograph, the first girl I met when I moved here away from my empty family home. She was too good for me. The fourth and a half was an open relationship. But she started dating the jocks less and less and started hanging with the skaters more and more, and... until she loved me but wasn't in love with me. She was into some kinky shit. Stuff I'd see during work. That's actually how I got the porno gig to begin with.

I never knew if she'd show up in a dress or combat boots. I met her by chance at some bar or another when I was drunk enough to dance. She thought I was funny. I thought she was hot and dangerous and wanted her for my own. And I did. That was when I was on the rise. Sleeping with a hot freak, doing crazy shit, partying and skating until dawn, really being out there at clubs, and never sleeping. Like the Korova Bar, for instance. They used to know me there by name. Somewhere along the way the fear of adulthood kinda just hit the pause button...

That must have been when I stopped worrying about cash, and got complacent. She got bored and left. I cried and drank and Jase was patient. I kept the porno-techie job and made good cash during my epic sulking. So maybe I never stressed about money, or time, whatever. I took that wild ride for granted. I felt some sense of security staying home and safe from all the raw pain and rejection waiting out there, and now...

Now it's been so long that I pay to get in and don't know any of the bartenders. It was a random event, a cosmic joke, that the one night I decided to shuffle back into Korova, I met Trish. And now I wasn't the life of the party, though I thought I was. No, by that point I was the lurker in the corner, just a couple years creeping up on the ripe old age of thirty.

Oh, but anyway, the kinky one. Using Japanese rope bondage and standard handcuffs was about as boring as she got. I think I have repressed memories from that one. But I kept the handcuffs as a sort of totem, a sentimental keepsake to remind me of the crazy one that got away. Bad habit of mine. Get comfortable and then things kind of just... after that I settled down in the worst way.

Hence the three years of nothing. But Trish, something about her attitude, her face, the way she dressed and carried herself, something about that reminded me of all of them. Of course, Scott Two knew this as well, so I made sure to grab them while he slept soundly in my bed, sticky from all his push-ups and crunches.

Contemplating my plan, lying in bed and letting my knuckles trace the photographs of my exes. Each lover defined a different life. Been years since I had to hastily cover up these photos with a Ninja Squad X poster or use the couch. But these faces, smiling, for me, and only me, from innocent and we'll be together high school sweethearts, to rebounds, to experiments, and all the blank spaces in between. I'm not sure any of these women would be interested in the Scott who kept them on the wall. I'm a new Scott. I'm not sure what I think about this Scott snoring next to me.

Scott Two finally woke up around midnight and joined us downstairs. I was stretched out on the couch, feet aimed at Jase. This forced Scott Two to squeeze in between us, at the end of the couch by the radiator.

We cracked our beers and smoked our weed, but Jase and I didn't inhale.

"So like, where do you think you came from?" Jase asked as he faked the gasping inhales that made it seem like he was keeping the weed in his lungs, instead of his mouth. Soop, soop, soop, he went. Then a forceful whooshing exhale. "We know you died, and it was like... nothing happening. But what are you? You're like a dude, dude. But what kind of dude are you? You know what I'm saying, dude?"

"I was thinking about that," Scott Two said as he hit the joint long and strong. The smoke bloomed around his face when he spoke. "You know about string theory, quantum mechanics, all that stuff? Fringe science, the kind that says all of reality is contained inside every quark, so we're living in this hyper recursive fractal loop that our brains can't even comprehend?"

Yes, Scott Two, I'm aware that we research these things. I'm also fairly certain Jase cannot comprehend it either.

"Yeah, that shit's like, for anything to be possible, it all has to be possible," Jase said.

I sat up.

He continued, "There are no limits outside our senses, so we're ill equipped, in fact, in danger of hubris, to assume what constitutes reality can be perceived through our meager five senses. Pass that shit, dude."

Holy shit, Jase, what the hell was that? Maybe you should lay off the ganja more often.

"Yeah man, or even the... like the opposite, like reality is only inherent within our senses and interper... interpretation of them."

"Reality is subjective to perception," I interjected.

They glared at me.

"Anyway, Jase, listen to this... I mean... the scientific community has pretty much come to a con... con... consensus that... uh..."

"That you're some demon asshole sent to torment me?"

"Dude, that makes no sense," Jase said. "We already know he's not the dead you. No wounds, no rotting... I mean, you both smell kinda rank, but otherwise it's all good. He's no zombie."

"So he says."

"I know where I came from. I rose from the abyss, into a brave new girl." Scott Two suddenly shut it, reflecting his loss of sense, and starting giggling. "I mean new world... infinite realities." His head flopped back. He kept talking with his eyes closed. "I'm from the world created when you died in a shitty bodegegegega. Man, this stuff hits hard. You guys this high?"

"Totally."

"Yes."

"Ah, so the uh... the scientists, all over the world they agree on infinite realities. Every action and possible reality exists, and every time we do something, another is created where we didn't."

"So technically there is some reality where Trish and I are together?"

"Yeah. And one where you and Jase are together."

Jase crushed his beer can. "And one where we're all lizards? And one where cockroaches rule the earth 'cause of World War Three? And one infested with demon soldiers and their lords of the Outer Church, and one where the King of all Tears reigns, and we're all slaves? And—"

"And one where you're a girl," I said.

This went on. And on. Jase rolled blunt after blunt, kept the bong packed, and within two hours Scott Two was high out of his fucking mind and swatting at the thick, skunky haze, and what the hell he saw in it.

"It's like a pot sea!" he said, his eyes way past red and into crimson bursting mode. "You guys should so something 'bout that sea turtle laughing on your TV. He's laughing at us!"

"I'll drop kick it," Jase said. Damn, he was good at keeping up the act.

"So when we got shot at, I think like... I come from the reality where we did get killed. I mean, I know for a fact I died. I'm starting to... remember more. The feeling of half my head just popping apart like a flaming melon. The last sight of fluorescent lights as I fell back. Cold tile. Getting colder. Colder. Siiiiiiinking."

The handcuffs hidden underneath me became uncomfortable. "Did it hurt?"

"Yeah, but not like..." He seemed to be dozing off. "I can't explain it. We never felt nothing like that before, even when we had that skating accident."

Oh man, yeah. When we were fifteen. That was bad. "So this was worse than falling down a ten-stair and dislocating your shoulder, cracking your collar bone, and snapping the radial all at once?"

"Oh, yeah, hell yeah! But different. Like uh... I can't explain. It's like a color that doesn't exist, you know?"

"I saw one of those once. Yo, you wanna hit this again?" Jase handed the bong toward Scott Two.

"No, I'm good," Scott Two yawned. "You know, I've been thinking... I've been think... I've been..."

"Come on, one more hit," Jase said. "You some kinda pussy, bro?"

Sealed eyes and a snort. Hands clasped awkwardly. Scott Two was out.

Jase and I held our breath.

We locked eyes.

Nodded.

It's go time.

"What the fuck is this is?" Scott Two screamed. He tried to stand, pulled with all his might, but all those pushups hadn't paid off yet. There was no way he was getting away from the radiator. He raged and reached and swung at us. I didn't know we were capable of such aggression. "You goddamn psychos! Let me go!"

I'm a nice guy. I did leave the leopard fur skin on the handcuffs, just to make his struggling less painful. I mean, I'm not a monster. Jase and I stood before him, arms crossed. I pulled the cuff key out of my pocket and dangled it in the air, just above Scott Two's flailing reach. Jase had his kit set up on the floor behind us. Jase pressed the pedal to make sure his tattoo gun worked, then primed the needles and set up the ink.

"Calm down, you silly little shit." Jase pulled on his gloves. "This won't hurt if you chill out."

His eyes widened. He slowly sat down. "Hurt?"

"So we've been thinking," I said. "What happens when my eye heals? And how do we keep you from ruining my life?" I gestured grandly toward the door.

"You can't keep me chained here! That's illegal, you sons of bitches! It's downright inhuman!"

"For all we know, you're downright inhuman! But for now, do as Jase says and relax. We're not going to keep you prisoner."

"What are you gonna do?"

"You're going to get your first tattoo, Scott Two!"

"Tattoo? Why?"

"'Cause Scott doesn't have one, duh. If we tat you up, I can tell the difference between ya, and Scott can finally stop whining about you running free."

"It's beyond me, but god forbid you sneak out and rob an old lady or something. If you're marked and I'm not, I don't pay the price for you."

"And if I bang Trish and I'm marked, you can never feel her sweet—"

I slapped. It felt wrong, seeing my red palm print on my own face. He stared back, more in disbelief than pain. It changed into a glare.

"Just give him something small, unique, just distinguishable for a worst case scenario, so I can prove I'm not him."

"What the hell are you so afraid of?"

"Yeah, yeah, I'll do Scott Two up right," Jase said, hunched over. He stood up and looked at us. "Ya know, calling you Scott, and you Scott Two, is getting really fucking annoying. We should name him something else."

"Oh, I got that covered," Scott Two said, staring straight at the wall, his face tensed up in anger.

I stopped, just as I was rounding the corner to the stairs toward sweet sleep. We faced each other.

"You... you renamed yourself?"

"Yup." He grinned.

"That's very independent of you. So what is it?"

"Scott Alvin is a shitty name. Weak. From now on, I'm Rex Von Gehenna."

"Badass," Jase said. He stood up with his gun and gloves on. "Like some kinda metal singer or something. Or an emperor in a dark castle. Lava flowing like a waterfall and shit."

"Rex Von Gehenna? What the hell kind of name is that?"

Scott Two—er, Rex—kept smiling at me. His lips didn't spread enough, leaving only the tips of his teeth prominent. The skin around his eyes pierced me, with his head tilted down.

Waking up with an arm wrapped around me was so wonderful. Nice, warm flesh, hugging me close and keeping me warm. And as quickly as the thought came, I bolted up and fell off my bed.

"Holy shit!"

"What? What's wrong?" Rex asked, still half asleep. He was lying face down on the other half of my bed, his arm still stretched out flat where I'd been, and drooling on my Roxar the Barbarian pillow.

"What the fuck are you doing in my bed?"

He rolled over and smiled. "Oh come on, we both know we've thought about sleeping with ourselves, you narcissistic little sissy. Remember all that kinky shit we used to do with—"

"Yeah, well... Well... That's my bed, so get the fuck out!"

"No, it's our bed."

"No. It's not. Rex."

He caught himself making that angry face again, and then bit his lip. "So. Where am I supposed to sleep then? Scott?"

"The fucking couch." I turned away, rubbing my eyes and heading for the blinds. The left one seriously hurt as I swept the crust away. And it tasted like a rat died on the roof of my mouth. "Get out of here. I'm going back to sleep."

"Nope. You gotta go to the ATM. Rent's due today," Rex said, his voice now constantly flat and slow.

"You go this time. I'm tired. I didn't get to hang out with Trish and then sleep all day like you. Where is she?"

"No idea. Because I did your job. And I can't go out now, remember?"

I turned around and saw him holding his forearm up, shrouded in Saran Wrap smeared in black and red. He twisted it mockingly.

"Holy shit, what did Jase do to you?"

"Exactly what you asked him to."

"What the fuck kind of tattoo is that? It's huge! I meant something on your back, like a two or something!"

He gave that dead smile again. "Pick up some whey protein shake mix while you're out. I'm going back to sleep."

Bang bang bang! Jase's door stayed shut. Bang. Bang.

BANG!

The door ripped open. Jase shouted. "What? What the fuck is it?"

"The tattoo, that's the fuck what! What the hell were you thinking?"

His eyes widened a little more, and then he smiled. "Oh yeah, dude. That's a sharktopus."

"What the hell is a sharktopus?"

"It's friggin' sweet, that's what it is. Didn't you see that movie? Classic, man. Half shark, half octopus. Badass! I got the tentacles wrapping all up the forearm around his elbow, and the shark mouth all open and scary at the end of his wrist. Shaded it real nice."

"Exactly! Real nice, you moron! You covered his entire forearm with a fucking sharktopus!"

"Yeah?" He lit a cigarette, leaned on the doorframe, rolled his head back. "This moron did it for free, don't you forget that."

"Dude, I wanted you to give him something discreet! He's gonna break out again anyway! So yeah, now you can tell us apart in any scenario except for the giant fucking fact that we have the same goddamn face!"

Jase's lips curled down as his eyebrows pinched together. Yeah, Jase. Exactly. Oops.

"I just... I dunno, Scott. I got inspired and Rex thought it would be really hardcore..."

"Rex thought, huh? Jesus Christ!" I spun around, pulling at my hair. "Now we're gonna have to give him plastic surgery or something! Anyone who sees both of us at all will... I'll have to wear long sleeve shirts all summer!"

"Tell him to."

"Yeah, like Rex is going to listen to me."

Jase tapped his foot. Scratched his ass. "We could just kill him."

What?

"Are you serious?"

"No," Jase said. "Fucking lighten up, man. We're not murderers. Besides, Rex is chill as hell. You're the one that's been all aggro lately."

He had a point. What was I doing to myself? Growing more and more bitter and afraid. But I couldn't keep Rex chained to the radiator. Someday, this disaster was bound to come out. "Jase, it was supposed to be small, something that would help if our friends—"

"When the hell was the last time we saw them anyway, dude?"

CRASH.

"What the hell was that?"

"Who cares?" Jase said through the door as it swung shut.

I was halfway to my room when Jase shouted, "Rent's due today!"

Jesus, I know.

No surprise. My bed was empty. The window was open. My Lords of the Universe curtains blew inward as I gripped the ledge and stared down to the street. Gone already. No telling where he went. Maybe after Trish, wherever she was. Damn! I slapped my forehead. In all my worrying, I didn't even get that info. Rex and I have the same long legs, so he's fast. Even if I knew what direction he ran, I'd barely have any chance to catch him with his head start.

I sighed and flopped onto the bed. Damn it, damn it, damn it. I stared at the dusty trunk next to my bed, the handcuffs hanging off the post again, the childish posters, the cobwebs in the corner. The pile of laundry next to its twin, differentiated only by smell and stain. Stared at the pictures of my former lovers, taped against the wall beside my bed. One blonde, freckles. A redhead, leather jacket. A hot punk rock mess, yet with eyes that sang softly of hope and sorrow, if you were lucky enough to hear them. One with long black hair and smile wrinkles around her eyes.

And a tomboy, pierced lip and brow (and tongue). And the long, empty space beside them. A breeze blew through the window.

Alright, time to get back to reality. Go hit up the bodega's ATM. The Trish-less bodega... but I guess I could fit in a few pushups first.

"Sir, your eye is disgusting. You really need to get that thing checked out."

I looked away from the ATM as it spit the rent money out. His skin seemed to glow through the new bodega glass, white beard and hair almost divine.

"Seriously, sir. It's disgusting."

"Thank you," I snapped. "I didn't notice, through all the throbbing burning pain and... and..."

"I'm just pointing out you might need to have it looked at. Have you even cleaned it?" He grabbed packets of single-dose aspirin and a tiny bottle of hydrogen peroxide. He held them out. "If you don't take care of it, you might lose your vision."

"Why do you..." I stared at his hand. "How much?"

"Just take it and go see the doctor. You buy enough here. I don't need another customer dying on me."

"Thanks," I muttered. He was right. My head felt like a watermelon swollen with blood. I clutched my eye and ripped my hand away like it was on fire. How had I lost sight of this thing? "Hey, I could use another job. You uh, have medical coverage here?"

The bodega owner laughed. I put my hands on the counter and looked him in the eye.

"What's your name?"

"Roy Turken," he said.

I shook his hand. "Scott Alvin."

"You were here the night we got shot up? So lucky you and Trish didn't get hurt."

"Uh… I did," I said, pointing at the red line beside my eye. "Well, grazed. It's not mascara."

He laughed.

"You haven't seen a guy that looks a lot like me in here with Trish, have you? Like… he looks exactly like me, but his eye isn't all gunky."

He shook his head. "Not since the day she quit. Why, is he your twin?"

Damn.

"Yeah, he's related to me." I rubbed my bad eye.

"Scott, it's just a small wound now, but it's in a sensitive spot. If it gets infected and connects to your eye tissue… My brother lost most of his vision when he—"

"Thanks, Roy. Gotta go!" I shouted, already out the door.

Damn, pulse too quick. Sun is hot and bright, like it got a twin.

Now with a fistful of cash, the placid brownstone street seemed like a safe haven, just past the dark BQE tunnel. A black SUV passed, its bass thumping like war drums. Didn't notice my hands were shaking until it was past the red light. It only takes three minutes to walk home. I got there in one.

Hopped down the steps to our sheltered entrance, fished around for my keys….

Go ahead, take a guess. I pounded the door.

"Jase! JASE!"

The curtains above did not part. A cloud floated under the sun. Perfect.

"JASE, I FORGOT MY KEYS!"

The purple curtains fluttered, the window cracked open the slightest bit, and the keys fell, catching the sunlight for a blinding moment. As I bounded up the steps he spoke through the door, perhaps half asleep.

"Just slip 'em under the door. And the rent. And leave me alone."

Back in my own sanctuary, I searched for my keys. Checked my other pair of pants in the dirty pile, the shorts in the clean pile, my desk, under my laptop, the rug, under the covers, behind the vintage 1977 Rageosaur statue that the handcuff keys were hid behind, then under the pillow, then back downstairs. Tore the couch cushions up, snooped the cluttered table like Sherlock Holmes, checked under the couch, kitchen everywhere.

A chill wind whistled through my still open bedroom window. Motherfucker!

"You stole my fucking keys!"

"What up, Rex? Remember, keep that tat out of the sun."

"He stole my fucking keys!"

"I made copies." Rex was standing in the open door, the steps to the upstairs apartment barely visible from my reclined position on the couch, and the moon just barely visible above his head, glowing like a halo through the staircase bars. "And I paid for them."

"I got locked out of the house because you…"

Rex tossed the keys at me. I barely caught them before the copper tore into my face. They were fresh, gleaming, clean. I looked over at Jase, hunched over his bong.

"I want the originals."

"Fine, fine, fine."

He tossed them underhand. I threw the copies at him pretty hard. They bounced off his chest before he caught them.

Jase laughed, spitting up into his bong. "Who wants a hit?"

Rex must have had a busy day, because he was already snoring on the couch by midnight. Jase and I were in his room, a cave of teenage angst turned to young adult pride. The two windows were open, each of us dangling our legs into the Brooklyn air, letting the cool sandy brownstone slap at our calves. We'd burned through three joints already.

"He was out there. All day. With her."

"Who?" Jase coughed.

"Rex!"

"No, I mean who was he with?"

"Trish."

"How do you know that?" He took a long drag, his beard glowing red behind the joint's flaring cherry.

"I can smell her on him. Besides, where else would I be? I mean—"

"You can SMELL her on him? Dude, one, why were you so close to him, and two... when was the last time you even saw her? The drive by? Dude, that was like..." He counted his fingers. "I dunno, a few days ago. And before that? I hate to say it, bro, but it's not like he's cock-blocking you."

I almost heard my teeth grind. I glared at the moon. A perfect, white graveyard.

"You think she liked the sharktopus?"

"Fuck the fucking SHARKTOPUS."

"Scott, man, seriously."

"What?"

"You gotta get your head checked out."

"Why? Don't you think I got more important shit to deal with right now?"

"Your eye, dude! You gotta get your eye fixed. If pus starts coming out of that thing, I'm gonna drag your ass out of here."

"It's just a gash next to my eye. I got a lot of other things on my mind, Jase. There's some seriously weird shit going on, and I'm on the verge of losing it!" I kicked my heel against the wall. I might have growled before I tilted forward too much, because in a heartbeat Jase's paw was clutching my back, reaching across the divide and pulling me back. He's oddly fast.

"Dude, I'm worried about you," he said. Another drag. Puff.

40

"Well, between rent, internet, electric, water, heat, and metaphysical freak outs, I can't really afford the visit, let alone the procedure to fix it."

"Maybe you're right. It's just a nasty cut, no big deal. But it's real close to an important place, and if you don't deal with it soon, you're gonna like, maybe lose your sight or something." He scratched his chin, the joint pinched in his mouth raised triumphantly into the night air. "I mean, it'd be kind of bad ass to have one eye, I guess. But it'll fuck up your skating."

"When was the last time we went skating?"

He flicked his joint down to the sidewalk with his right hand, pulled out the next with the left hand.

"Point taken, point missed. We're even."

"Great. I made friends with the bodega owner today. His name's Roy."

"Boring…"

I gripped the window ledge tighter, staring at the fenced in garbage cans below. "Man, if I just jumped right now…"

"You'd break your ankles. And anyway, we got a problem."

"No shit, Jase. And your fucking octoshark didn't help."

"Sharktopus. Get it straight. Anyway… Rex, you know, he's kinda cutting into our stash."

I glanced over my shoulder into the inky black mystery of Jase's cave. Somewhere in there was a big bag of primo weed and we weren't exactly growing it.

"Yeah, and?"

"I mean, we smoke a lot. But Rex… Dude, just adding him stretches our supply. It's like smoking two of you out. But I also think he's been dipping into the stash."

No way. Cardinal sin. You don't sneak a sip from the Holy Grail.

"Impossible. Even I have no idea where it is. It's your only secret."

"YOU don't know where it is. You wouldn't snoop around my shit."

I bit my lip. That's not cool. That's really not cool. This guy is really starting to turn into something else if Jase is getting annoyed. Maybe now he gets it.

"Well then lock your door."

"Scott, you gotta say something to him."

"Why me?"

"It'll be good for both of you. And I'll knock him the fuck out if he speaks back to me and I might sort of kind of feel bad about it."

"Not if he keeps doing all those pushups."

"And also, he's got your skills, dude. If you double up on the porn work, you can buy a second laptop, double your income, he can pay for his share of the bud, and—"

"Alright, alright. I get the point. I'll talk to him about it tomorrow. Assuming I even catch him before he disappears."

"We can still kill him," Jase laughed. "Or lock him to the radiator again."

I reflexively reached down to my keys, where I now had the handcuff key looped as well, all dangling from my belt buckle.

"He made his own keys."

"Yeah, well, what would you do?"

"Very funny," I sighed. I rolled backward inside, onto Jase's waterbed and into the darkness. Maybe I should get rid of the handcuffs altogether. And the kitchen knives.

"I don't think what I would do really applies to Rex anymore. You think he's gonna listen to me? About the cash?"

"Dude, it's double money! Of course. He's still... kinda... you. So he's not totally stupid."

"Thanks."

"I'm saying, is all I'm saying. And get that eye checked out bro. It ain't glaucoma."

"Maybe Rex will pay for it."

Nightmares. A sea of lips and limbs locked, Trish's green eyes and soft hair falling over my face, but then it's not mine, and my eye melts out of my skull and its Rex's muscular arms wrapped around the small of her back, and Rex's tongue tracing the inside of her bottom lip, and Rex's chest pressed against her tits, and then they're a throbbing mass of flesh, a fucking octopus, and a shark is just waiting behind them, waiting for me to break it up. Floating in the darkness, one eye closed, watching. I woke up sweating, standing over Rex, in real life, one of his arms behind his head, the other in his boxers, snoring like a baby in the bare moonlight.

I woke up with wicked beer shits and the toilet was completely clogged. It didn't matter who hit it first. Jase, Rex, inconsequential. They were both gone by sun up.

Unusual.

Jase must really need the money to be sitting at the tattoo shop before noon. I sat on the couch, coding away at my laptop. I usually end up squinting after an hour or two of checking lines of HTML and trying to be numb to all the hot idealized sex— well, male idealized, as the last ex taught me. Jesus, how long ago was that? Staring at the ceiling made me realize I was clenching my left eye shut. I left the laptop on the couch and went into the bathroom.

The damned smell… but I refused to unclog either of their shit. I clenched both eyes and poured a small bit of hydrogen peroxide down the left side of my face. Shouldn't burn that bad. Am I getting too sensitive?

As I came back downstairs, the door opened.

And in they came, together.

"Well, what do you think?" Rex asked. His arms were wide and jubilant. And his head was shaved. He had a mohawk.

"I was thinking he should dye it," Jase said. "Like leopard spots or something old school."

"Yeah, die," I said. "You two go on a date or something?"

"Nah, I bumped into him on the way back from the tat shop," Jase said, slipping under Rex's arm, spinning 180, and flopping into his chair. I think he lit a joint mid-motion…

"Jase and I talked about doubling down on the web maintenance," Rex said. "It's a great idea. Why don't we order a new laptop tonight, get it over-nighted. No doubt we'll be able to afford it. It was his idea."

"Yeah, that'd be a good start," I said. "And you can pay for the pot you've been pinching. And whichever of you jackasses left the toilet clogged can get up there and fix that. I've been holding this in all morning."

They looked at each other like puppies accused of eating the trash.

"Why didn't you do it then?" Rex asked.

My stomach burned fiercely. It was a tight competition for which irritated me more.

"I don't give a shit which one of you did it. Whoever clogged the toilet is gonna be the one who cleans it up!"

"I'll get right on it," Jase mumbled.

Rex kicked the door shut behind him.

"Mom and Dad would have killed us if they saw this haircut," Rex said. He flopped onto the couch and kicked his feet up on the table.

There's no proof I spoke, but something between us shut him the fuck down. He seemed to shrink into the couch.

"Um, I mean… they would have…" he mumbled.

I stood up.

He shut up.

I couldn't get over it. He's sitting there, with my face, my moles, my nose, my eyes and chin and lips, and almost all of my memories. And now a mohawk and a tattoo running up his already bigger forearm, and I have to admit, despite his zealous stupidity, Jase did an amazing job. Wait a second... "Is that my Iron Guillotine tank top?"

"Yeah. Duh."

"Yeah, let's get that laptop and pile on the clients. Then you can get your own fucking clothes."

"No arguments here!" Rex said, flopping onto the door side of the couch. Great, now I can't lay across the whole thing. "It's not like yours are gonna fit me soon anyway."

"So you bitched at me about talking to Rex and then you went ahead and did it anyway?"

"Well fuck it. You did nothing, as usual. Actually, he brought it up first. He's kinda smart like you, dude. He was kinda mad about it. Actually said sorry."

"He apologized?"

Jase leaned back on the tar pit grit of our roof. The sun was setting, shooting its final golden rays out as we welcomed the night. Our legs dangling over the brownstone, higher than the previous night. The feeling of black rust caked my palms. Never got used to climbing the fire escape. Another one of those things guaranteed to always hold you up and I just never bought it. I hold on too tight, always end up with these red flecks of rust crusting my palms.

Below us the streetlights stood stoic and red. They should be orange, but... no, they were red. The sidewalk was orange, the glow of our neighbors' windows just yellow eyes looking right through us.

Jase passed the joint.

"Whatever, Scott. It's not like you were really gonna confront him anyway."

"How do you know that?" My smoke exploded across his face by accident. "I got him to buy the laptop downtown. He's downstairs working this very moment."

Jase squinted and scrunched patiently through the smoke cloud. "You were REALLY gonna confront him?"

I turned away. Stood up, walked toward the backyard side of the roof, around the TV cables and rooftops' weird frozen waves. Stared down at the mini-ramp, the one Jase and I had to steal bits of plywood and cut from internet instructions to get just the right transition, the money we saved for Masonite, the hand painting of it. A small ramp, three feet high and eight feet long, just barely wedged in between the fences of our "back yard." It was lumpy now. Soggy. Neglected, forgotten. It took six months to put together. It was a hand built temple. Our child. Been years since we skated it.

"It's a damn shame," he said, scaring the shit out of me and nearly sending me over the edge. Jase caught me again.

"Yeah, we put so much work into it."

"Didn't even feel like work."

"When did we start neglecting it? We totally let it rot. I mean, it's not even covered by a tarp."

"Yeah, dude."

"Didn't cover it in the snow or rain in years. We really screwed up something special."

"Yeah, dude."

We simultaneously folded our arms, pondering how both of us could let something so precious and unique turn to rusty coping and soggy wood.

"Remember when we stole the coping from that construction site?" Jase asked. "We had to try to balance those damn pipes while we bombed that hill downtown? Oh my god, if we wiped out that would have been it. I couldn't have skated that fast WITHOUT the giant metal rod."

I laughed. I laughed so hard my eyes got wet, remembering Jase, teetering ahead of me, knocking a car's side mirror off with the huge metal pipe he was cradling as we streaked down the empty night street toward downtown square. Each of us cradling our half of the coping. A metal pipe eight feet long, stolen in the dead of night from some condo in construction, barely keeping our balance as we sped through an already deadly activity. Man, if we even passed a cop car we were done for. So young, and stupid, and fun.

"We got what's his name to cut it down for us," I said. "And that first day we skated it. Finally. After all that work. Those killer barbeque skate jams almost every weekend. What happened to all those guys? Mikey Meatloaf, Rotten Yellow Bones, Tim, Spitface, Boardlord, James, Nosebone? All those bros? Annika, Marlene, Desiree?"

"They just kinda stopped calling," Jase said. "And we stopped too. Everything kinda just... slowed down. Hell, we were what, 22 or something back then?"

He took an endless drag. Had enough time to pull out two cigarettes, light them off the joint cherry, and pass me one.

"Twenty-two... we've lived here a long time," I said. "It's gotten—Jase, it's gotten boring."

"Yeah, I think so."

I stared down at the dying ramp. Dying but not dead. "Been seven or eight years now."

He nodded.

We did what people do. We stood side by side and smoked our little passive aggressive wishes for death, and stared down at our glory days.

"You know... it's warped, but we could skate around that one hole. There's just enough light. And we could spin around the lamp in the kitchen to face out. The coping will stay in place if we don't jam it too hard..."

I looked back at Jase.

He had a kid's smile, all teeth and big ears.

You never forget those sounds. The ones particular to who you are. The ones outsiders never hear, but catch you like a dog whistle. For my dad, it was pigskin slapping into calloused hands. For us it was polyurethane wheels, seven layers of plywood, the distinct roll, acceleration, a pause, and then, clink, crush, slash, metal on metal. Sounds so violent but movements unique to each dancer, each person skating with their own odd grace and style.

It's funny... A lot of skaters don't dance, but the key to really expressing yourself is all in the movement of hips, knees, and shoulders. But you never get concussions, compound fractures, or broken ankles from dancing. I think. Come to think of it, when was the last time—

"Dude!"

WHAM. Too late. Masonite too soft under my ass, the side of my head hot and wet. Somehow I boardslid right across the whole length of coping, but right into a tree branch.

"Guess you got taller, bro."

I rubbed the left side of my head, looked at the blood, blinked. Left side a little blurrier but still workable. Yeah. Woke me up. This is it. The pain. You gotta pay to play. It works you up, gets the blood pumping, the primate dancing. You either get back on deck and drop in again, or go cry on the flatground.

I got on my feet, did the little bird step hop up the ramp's transition, and back onto the deck that barely held us. Jase dropped in, a little shaky, but each blunt made us more confident and quicker, forgetting the steps and just hearing the music in our heads.

Nothing fancy. No baroque orchestra. Just a nasty jazz solo. We'd both lost our smoothness over the years, but not the instinct. Within an hour, our eyes were red from smoking but wet with joy, and the blood was crusted to my skin, matting my hair down, and it felt right. This is the right kind of sticky.

Rock to fakie. Board slide. 180 to disaster. Fifty-fifty. Rock and roll. Deep rock to fakie. Frontside carve. Backside disaster. Fakie shuv-it to crook stall. Crailtap. A friggin Crailtap! Holy shit, Jase! We fed off each other's energy, willing cannibals, and it felt like a hundred girls watched through the chain link fence instead of yapping dogs and pissed off old men. The sounds… ka-klunk, kssssh, clack, thrum, ka-klunk, ksssh, thwhap, BAM. Laughter. Clacking the boards against the coping to keep our spirits up.

The second floor window slid open. The one over my bed. Rex craned his mohawked head out. Blaring yellow light framed his dark figure around the purpled brownstone.

"Sup guys? Sesh?"

"Yeah!" Jase shouted before I could stop him.

"Dude…"

"What?" Jase asked as we heard Rex slide the window shut. "Dude, he's not that bad. Let's see who skates better."

I tried not to smile.

"He's got all those muscles now, he might have better stamina."

"Might make him tighter though," I said, twisting around and spinning 360 on my board. I did a nice two-wheel manual across the patio, even over the cracks. It was like having my youth slip right back into my bones.

"Beer break! Time to praise Jah."

We sat down on white plastic chairs, grip tape down, staring at the scratches on our deck graphics. Skulls and blood and monsters and all sorts of childishly awesome things we'd ground away. Artwork destroyed. Sand mandalas.

Rex stood there by the little ramp, my bright orange old school toxic board under his arm. In this weird half-light he almost looked… like Rex. He was a little bulkier. His torn off jeans hugged his legs tighter than mine. His hairy calves were actually calf muscles instead of bones. He'd even bought his own shirt, red and black striped short sleeve. Kinda lame, but not something I'd ever wear. Even his neck was thicker.

"How long has it been since you popped up?" I asked.

Jase passed the blunt to Rex. "Over a week for sure, maybe two and a half. Not really sure."

"The days just melt away, huh?" Rex said. He took a mighty hit then continued to pass it around the circle. "Time flies when you're having fun."

I passed the blunt to Rex. The damn thing was so small our fingertips nearly touched. For a moment the dried out tobacco leaf linked us, and a moment later, the moment was broken. I did my best to pinch the little bastard and pull smoke through.

"How much work did you get done?"

"Enough to pay you back, easy," Rex said, lightly backhanding Jase on the shoulder. "Sorry about snooping around, bro. It's been hard, you know, dying and stuff."

"Yeah, whatever. Get me the cash before Friday. I gotta do another pickup."

Jase has been locking his door. I know because he only does it to whack off, and now he locks it all the time. I'm pretty sure he's not whacking off all the time. Pretty sure.

"How about a game of S.K.A.T.E.?" Rex suggested, looking me dead in the eye.

I thought about all my tricks. I could cheese him out. Variations of tricks, ollie, then nollie, nollie shuv-it front side and backside, big spin, half cabs, boneless, 180 boneless, fakie shuv-it… more than enough moves to make him choke at least once, then hit the endless chain and make him spell out S.K.A.T.E.

Make him a loser.

"Dumbasses! You both know the same tricks!" Jase said.

"Not necessarily," I said. I cracked my neck, then stomped the blunt roach out on the patio. I was all warmed up. Rex hadn't skated since... well, not even since the last time I skated. Ha!

"Best two out of three, Scott?"

"I got winner," Jase said, leaning back. He pulled a beer out of thin air.

Crack.

"Best two out of three, Rex," I smiled. "You go first."

Show off. He busted his ass on his first try at a kick flip. Idiot. We hadn't landed that trick in years. I did it switch stance. For the first time ever. Ha.

My turn to set the tricks.

I kicked his ass twice.

Back in the kitchen, dripping sweat like gods, my chest felt as big as Rex's looked. Rex and I fell into position on the couch, myself by the radiator and steps, him by the exit. Jase's ass stuck out past the open fridge door. He tossed two beers at us blind, and we caught them the same. Rex rested his on the underside of his board and cracked it. I rolled my board under my feet on the carpet, savoring the feel of my toes hot and stuck together, having earned it. Rolled my socks down a bit, felt the sweat evaporate. Cracked my beer. Jase ambled in with a case under his armpit and a fat, fat, fatty blunt in his hand.

"That was fucking awesome!" I said.

Jase high fived me.

"For sure," he said. He reached out and gave Rex a fist bump. "Nice try, Rexy, but Scott's got you cooked."

"For now."

Jase concentrated very hard. "Hey, isn't Rex a name you give to dogs and shit?"

I felt good. The air was hot, the beer was cold, the night was pure amber peace.

Still feeling amped from the skating, I went upstairs to see if any porn sites needed new backdoor protection from hackers. Why don't they put their skills into hacking the Pentagon or something? Guess there's more money selling access to this bullshit. My laptop was open on my desk, and Rex's was right beside, a newer version, all black. With a camera built in and wireless everything updated to awesome version 2.0. But mine was still fine. I was leaning over, clicking through the program, looking at what sites needed what maintenance and logging some hours in, and Rex appeared beside me. I nearly knocked my old, silent phone off the desk. The bill for its service plan fluttered to the rug.

"Jesus Christ! You scared the shit out of me!"

"Good game. You're still a good skater. Not bad for someone who's sat on his ass for years." He slapped my shoulder, then gripped it a bit too tight.

"Yup." I shrugged him out.

"Hey, check this out," he said. He leaned over my computer and started pulling up web pages. "Trish told me all about her new job."

There she was. Smiling and looking up at me, surrounded by hairy legs and cocks and just utterly soaked. Completely, totally, covered. For the first time in all these years of working with images and videos like this, I felt ashamed.

"When the hell? How could Trish—"

"How could Trish what? What are you thinking, Scott? Are you JUDGING her?"

I shook my head and pushed him away. "No, just—just shut up, Rex."

"Well, if you really wanna know, I brought up our job that day I spent with her in the park, back when she still thought I was you." Rex smiled. He clapped me on the back. "One thing led to another, and YOU gave her a contact in one of the east coast offices. This is your work, Scott! Trish got her big break because of you! And she loves it, the kinky little bitch! She's just like our last—"

"MY last girlfriend." I had to look back. I should have killed Rex on the spot, but I felt some infinite pit. I could spend the rest of my life staring at her in these porn shots, covered in cum, while she looked... happy. I know not all porn stars are drug addicts or abused, but... What I really knew now was that I didn't know HER. Didn't know she had that tattoo on her ass, or the tramp stamp, or that she was pierced in all those spots. The only thing I knew was what I wanted Trish to be.

"And you... still like her?" I asked.

"Hell yeah, man! We love this kind of shit," he said, wrapping his arm around my shoulder.

I shrugged him off. "I'm not so sure about that."

"Aren't you mad?"

"What?"

He looked disappointed.

"Why aren't you mad at me? Look what I did! Look what I turned into with your face!"

I just shook my head. "I don't give a fuck, man. You still like her? You'd still sleep with her after this?"

"Hell yeah, I would."

Actually, I probably would too. I'm no saint. But still...

"Well, so she's happy, right?"

"She loves it. You're not even gonna ask? It's not eating you alive?"

"Ask what?"

"If I've fucked her!"

"Rex, I don't care."

I walked away, down into the living room, and flopped on the couch. Jase was staring at me. He'd obviously heard everything.

"Dude, that shit is whack."

"Yup."

"You really don't care?"

"I'm tired." I curled up into the cushions.

I was woken by Rex bounding down the stairs. I stretched across the couch, relishing the feel of sweat making my shirt into a second skin, the dripping on my legs, my hot, sore feet. I yawned, looked at Jase hitting his bong. His eyebrows knotted up as he spotted something Rex was hiding behind his back.

"How long was I asleep?"

"Like 20 minutes," Jase said. "Rex. What are you…?"

Rex towered over me and slowly revealed his secret. He tossed it over my head, catching it just before it hit my face. Letting it spin and slap back into his grip. Thwap. Thwap.

"What the hell is that?" I said. I felt a fever rising, a thousand demons crawling across my skin.

"It's a football, dipshit," Rex said.

"I know what the fuck it is. What the FUCK are YOU doing with it?"

He stopped tossing it. I sat up.

"I want to play catch. Jase, you down?"

"As long as I can play sitting here, yeah, whatever."

I already knew the answer, but… "Rex, where did you get that football?"

His answer was barely audible over the rush of blood tunneling through me.

"You know where."

"I didn't know you gave a shit about football," Jase said. He coughed up smoke.

"We don't," Rex said. He tossed the football over his shoulder without looking. I couldn't react fast enough.

Thump.

It landed safely in Jase's lap, and the precious glass bong was still balanced on Jase's knee like a child, his grip firm. He looked over the football. "Dude, this motherfucker's old."

"It was our dad's." Rex smiled a shark's grin.

"That's not true," I said. I stood up, nose to nose with Rex. I saw red, I saw fire, I felt fire. He wants a fight. He wants me to lose it. He wants to beat me down. He wants to win. So he wants a fight? He's going to get a fucking fight.

"Rex, that was MY dad's football. Not OUR dad's. You had no right opening that trunk!"

He smiled, all teeth, no eyes.

"Hey, chill out, I just wanted to play catch. After all, skating was so much fun."

Jase tossed the football. I saw it arc up and over Rex's shoulder, and as the white stitches spiraled, I saw my dad, my mom. MY dad. MY mom. It landed perfectly in my arms, cradled against my chest like Dad taught me.

Rex was fast. He snatched it right out of my grasp and held it over my head. So he wants me to jump up for it? Like a dog? Like he's my big brother?

"Scotty, don't you wanna play?"

"Rex, I'm going to say this once." My heart was thudding louder and louder, almost couldn't hear myself. "You have no right to my life. NO RIGHT. You're not me, REX. And he was NOT. YOUR. FATHER."

"Aw, are you gonna cry?"

"No. I'm going to kill you."

"What?"

The second my fist hit his stomach, I realized how many sit-ups he'd been doing. I bent my wrist on impact. It hurt. He didn't even flinch. He was still holding the damn football above us. Smiling like the fucking sharktopus on his beefy forearm.

"Nice shot, tough guy. Too bad you don't fight as well as you skate."

Rex spun and fired the ball at Jase. It spun like a rocket, right at Jase's face, which was pressed down to the bong. He had his lighter in hand, ready to spark up the bowl. Seconds stretched into minutes as I waited for the pigskin to crush Jase's nose.

The bong crashed to the floor. The old weed water drenched Jase's lap, ran down his leg to the floor where the weed lay wasted. Northern lights, too. Expensive stuff.

And my dad's football was in Jase's hand, a perfect grip, right around the stitches. His head was still lowered, his back hunched.

"I'm fucking serious," Jase said. His eyes rolled up to us, his head still craned down. "Back off. Leave Scott alone."

Rex stared at him, then back at me. I was rubbing my wrist, but I was still stood nose to nose with him. Rex's grin faded. He shrugged.

"Okay, okay. Geez, don't be so uptight. Throw me a beer."

Neither of us did.

I was back upstairs, carefully packing the football into the trunk. I squatted there staring around the room. The whole room was a trunk. All these things I loved, they were all... old. Things I loved as a child, and yes, still loved now, but they didn't inspire nostalgia this time. They were anchors. The posters, the toys, the vintage this and that, the collectibles... they anchored me to reality, to sanity, to... complacency. To this place. I started to get this weird idea.

I went back downstairs. Rex was laid out silently on the couch. Jase was sitting, hands folded. Very weird. I was more afraid Jase was about to pounce on Rex and make good on his joke about killing him.

"Rex."

He looked up at me as if nothing had happened.

I continued. "Rex, why do you hate me?"

His eyes grew. He sat straight up.

"Why do I hate you?"

"Yeah. What is it, man? Why aren't you content with getting a new life, getting the girl, living at my place and being friends with Jase? What is it you're missing?"

"I hate you because you hate me."

What the fuck?

"I…" Bit my lip. "I don't hate you. I'm just… uh…" My eyes were watering up. "I might be a little jealous of you. You're a dick. You're an asshole. But you do have a better life."

"You're supposed to hate me. I stole your girl. I stole your life!"

I laughed at him, dismissive. Looking down on him on the couch, I crossed my arms and sighed. Hand shielding face, speaking through fingers. "Fuck it, Rex. You can have the girl. But you can't have my life. You're not me anymore. And I won't live hating myself."

"He's not you," Jase put his hand on my shoulder. "You're both losers, but you're totally different losers!"

Rex laughed, head hanging. I fought back a smile.

He spoke to both of us. "Why don't we go outside and skate some more, huh? The three of us, let's just… let's spark up a blunt and have another session? Cool?"

No one spoke.

"Cool," I said.

"Cool," Rex said. He was looking at the ground. He looked up at me. Was that… shame? "You guys aren't gonna jump me or something? Whack me in the back of the head with your boards and kick my ribs in?"

I laughed, scratching the back of my head. Jase was already lumbering outside, beer and board in hand.

And that sealed the deal.

We skated for a second time that night. Things felt different. Calmer. But I felt bad, and not because of Rex. I felt bad for Jase, because he didn't know what I was really thinking, and I didn't know when or how to tell him.

What a long night. We were back in the living room, but there was a Zen feeling to it all. Rex went down to the bodega and picked up some microwavable pizzas. When he got back, Jase rolled three joints and passed three beers.

"Damn, it's starting to stink in here," Jase said. He looked around the room as if he'd never seen it before. "There's like way too much man sweat in this room."

We were chowing down on our pizza when I put my slice down and said. "Hey guys. I've been thinking. I'm—"

Bzzzzzzz. BZZZZZZZZ.

"What the fuck is that?" I leapt from the couch.

BZZZZZZZZZZZZZ!

"It's upstairs," Jase said. He slowly kept his gaze pierced at the staircase as he reached for a porno mag. He rolled it up. "This could be it, boys. The big one! Giant mutant hell bugs!"

"It's not a bug..." Rex said, his voice higher pitched than normal. "Let me—"

BZZZZZZZZZZZZZ!

It was a vibration. I walked right upstairs to my bedroom. Sure enough, there it was on my desk. Right next to Rex's new laptop. My cell phone, many years out of date. No internet connection, no texting, no pics or nothing. And no ringtone.

The last time I heard that phone ring, that was... uh... the last time this phone rang and... I uh... I found out about Mom and Dad.

I stared at Dad's old college trunk at the foot of my bed. Covered in stickers and slogans and images as alien to me as the ones that caked my walls would someday be to my future child. I sat down on the trunk.

Stared at the vibrating phone, waiting for it to shuffle right off my palm. Bit my lip. No one has this number. Not unless the old, old, old gang heard us skating from god knows where. I kept the bills paid for that phone, never really sure why. Always kept it visible, right beside me on the desk, silent.

Bzzzzzzzzzzzzzzzzzzz!

Held my breath.

Rex was standing in the doorway. He wouldn't enter. My vision grayed out, then came then back.

BZZZZZZZ—

Flicked it open.

"Hello?"

"Um, hi… Is this… Scott?"

It was a girl. Not just any girl.

Holy fucking cock and balls yes awesome oh my—

"Yeah. Yeah, it's Scott. Hey, what's up?" I croaked. "What's… what's good, Trish?"

Rex muffled a laugh.

"Oh, I'm so glad I got the right number!"

"Me too!" I said. I immediately smacked the side of my head. Stupid. Looked up to see Rex still frozen in the doorway. "How ya doin'? I haven't seen you since we almost got shot up, oh, I mean… uh…"

Rex mouthed "the bar."

"I mean the bar. That was cool?" I glared at Rex. "How's your boyfriend?"

"I totally ditched that fucktard I was dating, but I guess he already told you," she said.

"Oh, yeah, I heard." I glared at Rex. "So like, how are you gonna make money now if you don't come back to the bodega? I

59

miss… I miss seeing you there. It's so gloomy, especially since it got all shot up. Ha."

"Oh, I'm so over that shithole. I took your advice. I got much a better gig now. It's a little… weird, but way less hours, WAY better pay. Better… ah… perks? Ha! You know. Anyway…"

"Hey, how'd you get this numb—"

"Your cousin Rex said he was staying at your place while he was in town, but he lost his phone. He said to call yours to reach him. Is he there?"

I swear to god I could set him on fire if I thought hard enough. Next thing I know, the left side feels like hot liquid and my peripheral vision is shrinking and Trish's voice is distant and slow and somehow now I'm standing and my hands are falling to my side and Rex is still dead still.

I snapped the phone shut.

"You. Mother. Fucker."

"Scott…"

"You motherfucker. There's just no end to it! How many second chances do you want, you fucking moron?"

"HEY!" He was holding me back with one arm. "Listen, Scott, we—YOU—had your chance and failed. Listen, BRO, you can't be absent for practice and play for the team."

That was Dad's old saying. His hand would be on my shoulder, just like Rex's was now. That was MY dad's saying. The phone hit the floor.

I swung.

I missed.

Slammed my right hand right into the right door-frame. Rex was already halfway down the hall, still facing me. He backed into Jase, who was standing with a beer in each of his hands, brow furrowed.

I shook the pain away.

I picked up the phone. Stared down at it. Looked up at Rex, who was saying something to Jase. I threw it as hard as I could at his nose.

He caught it.

I fell to my knees. Couldn't even cry.

Rex was right. He was right. He was right.

I heard him dialing her number, the one I didn't know because I was absent for practice.

Rex was gently pushing past Jase as he focused on the phone and moved downstairs. Jase was watching me, unsure. I stood up, wiped my brow. Jase met me halfway down the hall, where the bathroom door stood across from his, and the swirl of smells made a toxic spiral.

"Gonna clean up that wound?" he asked.

"Yeah. I'm gonna clean up."

I poured the last of the hydrogen peroxide all over the left side of my face. Bathed in the burn of it. Cleansing burn.

Jase punched me in the shoulder. I spun around and dropped the bottle.

"Good job at S.K.A.T.E., man. It's tough to beat yourself! Remember all those old games where you gotta fight your shadow clone before the final boss? They always do that. They all made you fight yourself before the big bad last boss finally showed up. And then it would be some totally weird shit out of left field, like a dog with a machine gun in a helicopter, or—"

"Jase, I didn't beat myself. I beat Rex."

I heard him from downstairs.

"Trish? Yeah, it's Rex, babe," His voice was rougher than mine. "Hey, yeah, sorry about that. Bad connection."

Yes, Trish is coming over to see Rex.

"Well, now you'll get to spend some time with her for real! Dude, she's a freak!" Rex said, bouncing on the couch. "One time she just picked up this double ended—"

"I. Don't. Care."

"You're harshing my mellow." Jase was sitting in his corner throne, bong in lap. The happy Buddha, but without his smile.

"Harshing your mellow? Seriously?"

"Uh, okay… How about you're a pervert and a dickhead?" Jase said. "I seriously don't see how Scott spawned you."

"You forgot cock-blocker," I added. I was slumped into the couch's corner, arms crossed, legs, crossed, every muscle in my body tensed, tendons and fibers ready to burst apart like rubber bands beyond their—

"Limits, bro. There's gotta be some limits," Jase said. His face was still unchanged.

"What are you talking about? Scott said he's cool with it," Rex said, slapping my shoulder. "And maybe I'm a dickhead, but I'm not a cock-blocker. Scott didn't do shit, and he even said it's cool for her to come by."

It's true. I did say she could come over. Come over to see my "cousin Rex." But I never said I was COOL with it.

"Maybe you wanna watch, eh?" Rex elbowed me, bouncing on the couch, dust puffing up around him. "Or some weirdo three-way. Imagine that, a Scott at each end of her? She'd be into it!"

"There'd only be one Scott," Jase mumbled.

"What?" Rex shot.

"I said you're lucky you paid me back so fast, 'cause you're kinda starting to be a pain in the ass."

"Yeah, well, let me know when it hurts bad enough and we'll see if I can't kick that pain right out of your fat ass."

Jase's eyes came from another world. My vitriol shrank between my legs. And just as suddenly... Jase ripped an epic fart. No one could keep up the tough guy act after that.

"Jesus Christ, man! Did a chipmunk die in your ass?"

"Fuck you, Rex. Bong hit?" Jase asked, head tilted, eyebrows high and happy.

"So when is she coming over?" I asked.

Rex exhaled the smoke slowly, dragon like. "Takes about a half hour as long as the train's running right."

WHAT?

"Dude, she's coming over right now?" Jase asked. He sat forward, nearly spilling the bong as he snatched it back. He pulled a cigarette from behind his ear and began puffing on it intently.

"Duh," Rex said. "What did you think I meant, for Thanksgiving?"

"I thought you were asking if it was okay if she came over in general. Not now! Not while I'm HERE!"

"Huh? Who cares if you're here?" he said. "She ain't gonna give a shit. And I thought you didn't."

Jase, now properly speaking in a low and even tone, dispensed his wisdom:

"Dude... dude, you are a DICKHEAD."

"I better take a shower," Rex said. "All that skating really got me pumped up. Gotta calm down and make sure this DICKHEAD'S blood goes back to his DICK head. Faggots."

He laughed. And laughed. And we did not.

"No, I gotta take a shower," I said, scrambling towards the stairs.

Made it! I slammed the white door behind me, the faintly pee smelling towels whipping out past my head from their hooks. I could hear Rex downstairs saying something about how chicks dig man sweat anyway. Pheromones. Fuck it. I'm taking a shower. But I needed my shower sandals first.

I shuffled into my room, looking for the little foot shields that kept the weird brown fungus in our tub from creeping between my toes. What the hell is that stuff anyway? I dumped bleach on the scum once, and it was back the next day. Nefarious bastard.

I found the sandals next to my bed, ready for my morning routine. Moonlight lasered in through the blinds, pinpointing my pillow. I stared at the large bed, the three pillows, the rumpled sheets. No. No way. I know what he's going to ask. Assuming he even asks at all.

I dropped to the floor, fishing out all those show-off magnum sized condoms. I scooped them up and tossed them out the window. Onto our sidewalk. Great. That's going to ruin some stroller pusher's morning. I slumped against the wall. Right next to the heater that once burned me when I fell into this exact same position the last time I answered that FUCKING PHONE.

Thud, thud, thud.

Passively cracking my head against the wall made my eye hurt a little less. Oh! Of course. He'll know where the real condoms are. What am I even thinking, he'll have his own. He's probably already... Why do I even... Jase's shadow slipped in.

"I thought I didn't care when it was all an, an, idea."

"Fuck that shit," Jase said from the doorway. He leaned against the frame, his elbow balancing him and his hand behind his head.

"You look like you have a giant triangle coming out of your head."

"You sound like your mouth's full of sand, dude."

Jase walked across the carpet, stepping over my action figures, and sat down in front of me. I didn't look up. He didn't speak. He didn't light a joint or cigarette.

"Scott? Bro?"

"Fuck."

"Fuck."

"Farts."

"Piss."

Laughs.

"Can I have a cigarette?"

He sparked it himself and passed it over. The ash cloud burned, my throat burned, my eye burned, everything burned.

"Jase, isn't fire supposed to be cleansing?"

"Uh... no, bro. Fire burns shit. Flames of hell, eternal suffering. Looks cool and badass as a motherfucker, but unless you mean clean as in completely erase whatever was there before—"

"Yeah, that's what I mean."

"Well, yeah, I guess you uh... Wait!" He clutched my arm. "You're not gonna set him on fire, are you?"

"No!"

"Seriously? 'Cause that'd actually be kinda cool."

"No, Jase. I'm not setting anyone on fire."

"What about the apartment? Please don't tell me you're gonna burn down our fortress."

"NO!" I shrugged his hand off me.

His eyes were still wide with this weird mix of fear and fascination. "Well, what are you gonna burn then?"

"Myself."

"Like that Buddhist dude? Pfffft. Boring. Besides, I thought you were gonna take a shower. Good luck, dude. If you manage to set yourself on fire in the shower, you deserve some kind of cosmic reward." He leaned back on his hands.

"I deserve one already. I got a cosmic punishment."

"Huh. Yeah, you know, maybe you already got your reward."

My cigarette lifted with my eyes. "What are you getting at?"

"Maybe your cosmic gift is sitting downstairs."

"Trish ain't here yet."

"Jesus's ass, man, you are fucking dense sometimes."

"You're telling me that Rex is… is… no, not getting shot in the drive by was a cosmic gift! You're way stoned, man."

"Well, yeah, but if you think about it…"

Knock, knock.

Not at my door. Out the window.

My eyes were glued to the windowsill. Down by the stairs, leading to the stairs down to our door, the top of a brown head with a green streak. And a new blue one.

"You gonna go let her in?" Jase asked. He was looking down, lighting his own stogie.

"She's not here for me."

I slipped on my just clean enough shower slippers and went into the closet sized bathroom.

Staring at the green ooze caking the tiles… If we'd gotten rid of it before it hardened we wouldn't have this problem. It's too late now. Right? It's too late?

I waited for the sound of Jase returning downstairs, the muffled voices, one deep, one lazy, one soft and beautiful, before I drowned them out with burning water. Yup. Any doubts from before were dead. I knew for sure what needed to be done.

I did find a pair of clean pants, full of rips and holes and other cool tough guy things. I put on the tightest shirt I could find, an Ultra-Mandroid tee from when I was very, very young. It still fit, tight. Made my arms look a lot bigger. And clean socks.

Stood at the top of the staircase. I could hear them down there. When did we get twice as many stairs? When did the hallway get so dark… When did… my head… fuzzy… what's that… why am I sinking… why can't I see the…

Wake up.

Dude.

Wake up.

Whaaaa… Nooooo. Void. Quiet.

Yo, freak!

"Dude, wake up!"

The light burned, sneaking its way through the three titans crowded over me, all hands on knees, close enough to get a good look, but not too close. I felt my body all twisted and weird. Bent in ways that would make taffy scream. I slowly unknotted myself, realized I was at the foot of the steps, and Rex's mohawk, and Trish's face, and Jase, and, and… Trish's face.

"That was a hell of an entrance," she said. "Passing out and falling down a flight of stairs? You're lucky you didn't break your neck."

She was blurry but beautiful. A phantom on the left, a clear clean girl's face on the right. "I guess we're both ones for luck. Remember that poor dude from the drive by?"

"True that," she laughed. "He was a total shitdick anyway. Probably had it coming."

"Did he end up living?"

"I have no clue, dude."

"You alright, bro?" Rex said. Why was he smiling? WAS he smiling?

"Scott's shot 'cause he shredded like a mother fucker," Jase said. He stood tall and raised his beer to the ceiling. "You shoulda seen this dude, Trish. My man's gnar as all hell. He beat Rex at S.K.A.T.E. twice! Trounced him!"

"That's… great? Congratulations?"

I watched Jase clutch Trish's soft arms, bare but for her green shirt, as Jase tried to impress upon her how monumental a victory like that was.

"Beating someone in S.K.A.T.E. is ten times harder than like—"

"What is that, like H.O.R.S.E. in basketball?"

"Exactly! It's like, not just your shot. It's your style, your choice, your moves, your very SOUL is on that board!"

"Right. I'm gonna go make sure Scott didn't hurt his uh, soul, or whatever." She gave him the stink eye.

I stayed on the floor. She's coming. I cracked my neck, saw a roach scutter under Jase's chair, inches from my face. God, what strange temple must exist under there. I looked back to her, this girl I lusted for, closer now. I mean, she was really closer now, on one knee, her hand on my chest, looking me in the eye.

It was too much. Her hand made me feel sleepy, like her hands were... I don't know, awesome hands. Her green eyes, looking right into mine. In the right light you really can see your own reflection in someone's eyes, and this was the right light.

What I saw was a tired face, dark bags under my eyes, pale skin. A nasty red wound wrapping around my one bloodshot eye. The gray, fading eye. The vision itself was more blurred, as if it were a dream fading upon waking. A dream you swore in those half-life moments you'd remember, but knew in your heart would forget. I saw one dying, gray eye, fading away. But I saw my other eye beside it. Bright and brown, full of life, ready to move and take on all the world. I saw...

I saw.

Jase and Rex were talking above us, just muffled shadows.

I sat up slowly. "Who wants to smoke?" I smiled.

They all stared at me incredulously.

"What?" Rex asked.

"What's wrong? Dude, beer me, and spark one up." I smiled.

"Yo bro, you hit your head or something?" Jase asked.

"Probably," I said.

"He definitely cracked his dome," Rex said.

I was leaning on my elbows when the beer entered the room. I noticed that although my vintage Ultra-Mandroid shirt still fit my body's width, I forgot about length. It was now more of a belly shirt. I laughed inside. The beer passed from Jase, to Trish, to Rex, and then down to me.

We locked eyes. Neutral.

"You sure you're okay?" Rex asked. He tilted his head, squinted his eyes.

Trish's emerald eyes faded to green. Her smile stayed as coy and enticing as ever.

"Yup. Better than okay."

I've dealt with some weird shit.

I found out not all wounds heal, no matter how hard you try. I've been low on the highest points and vice versa, shredded my skateboard and looked death in the eye knowing the one in the short skirt was watching my every move and loved my sweat. I've been left handcuffed to a pipe in my ex's bedroom for over an hour while she left for "groceries," and I stared down a strap-on and didn't back away. And I found out someone always gets left out in a threesome. That you can't skate forever. I've been shot down, and shot up, and thrown sideways, and laughed when I should have cried, and cried from laughter. I smiled at bad jokes and walked alone in foreign alleys. I've been woken up and told about the party I missed the night before. I've worn women's underwear. Twice. I let my job and lust for easy money turn me into a shell of the Scott I liked. Had a hailstorm of bullets barely miss my head. I've flipped open a phone and felt the world shift beneath my feet and the sky laugh with fire. Found out death isn't as explosive as in the movies. And never opened my father's trunk since. Yes, I let dirty laundry and junk pile up on it, but never lost it.

And I've had my identity stolen.

And then discarded.

And so I watched, cross-legged on the couch, while that thief wooed the woman of my dreams, while my best friend laughed at their jokes. I gave Jase the "let's not cock-block" look and nodded that we should leave them on the couch. Jase silently mouthed "upstairs?" I shook my head no.

"Guess what?" I asked.

Trish was half in the bag, half in Rex's lap. Jase's eyes were crimson baseballs.

I was sitting on the floor, cross-legged, leaning against our analog TV. "My bed was killing me last night. I'm like... way too beat up. All the skating and passing out and getting trashed... You guys mind if, uh... Sorry, is it cool if everyone just leaves me down here? I'm really tired."

Yeah, they all stared in stunned silence. Trish a little less so.

"Just let me pass out on the couch. Leave me be. Leave me alone. Please."

They all got up slowly, zombies rising, unsure of their role in this strange new world. Jase hunched down before me, two cigarettes in his mouth, looking me dead in the bloodshot eye. "You sure you didn't crack your head open, dude?"

"I'm quite sure."

"Where are we gonna... Well, I mean..." Rex began. "I can't let Trish go home alone this late! And I'm pretty beat too. Where do we sleep?"

"Would you like to use my room?"

Trish was dangling around Rex's neck, her flimsy body clinging like a necklace to a totem pole. Rex was staring me down, almost... afraid. "You sure... cousin?"

"Yup."

"You're cool with me and Trish sleeping in your room? I mean... I guess there's room for—"

"Rex. Seriously. It's cool."

He looked at me like a dog confounded by its master.

"Hey, what are cousins for? Right?" I smiled. "Unless you wanna sleep in Jase's room and get all freaky-deaky. Lord knows it runs in the family, right cuz?"

"Nah, I'm good on that," Jase said. "I ain't into mohawks OR dickheads. Girl's cool, though."

"Gee, thanks," she said. "I'm so validated."

I shooed them away.

Rex carried Trish up the dark stairs toward my room, the light streaming out across them. Jase walked around the kitchen, clicking the lights out, paused at the final lamp above his personal throne.

"You want help getting to the couch?"

I stood, a puzzle slowly unfolding, creaking, cracking, content.

"I got it."

"Scott, are you... I mean..." He looked over his shoulder and saw the staircase pitch black, meaning my door was closed. "Dude, Rex is gonna bang her out in there."

I sighed, swallowed, hung my head, whatever image works for you.

"I know that. It's a little too late to put up a fight now. The game's over. Maybe I can at least get a good night's sleep in."

"And I'm not gonna wake up and find a bunch of bodies all over the floor? 'Cause that would be a bitch to clean."

"Ha, no. Trust me, man, he's tried everything he could. It's game over."

They fucked in my bed. More than once, as I heard lying awake all night on that couch. I stared down at my bed. His spunk and her cream coated my sheets. The smell of their sex, rank and oppressive and undeniable as crabs cracked on a beach shore, maybe for the first time, maybe not, but yes, many times.

They took a shower together in the morning, but they only had one pair of sandals. Gross. I heard them moaning through the streams of clean water, while I hopped up and down holding my piss outside. I eventually joined Jase in refilling the old empty malt liquor bottles downstairs.

I was coding on my laptop downstairs, Jase was sketching a new tattoo for a client, and Rex and Trish stood at the door.

"We're going to the park," Rex said. "Later, losers."

Trish waved limply. "Later, Jase. See ya, Scott. Thanks for the uh… hospitality."

"No prob. Have fun."

The door shut.

I put my laptop down.

"Jase."

"Yeah?" he didn't look up.

"Jason."

His pen ceased its furious scratching. He put it down, eyes wide and weird.

"Dude, what?"

"I'm leaving."

He was up and moving in circles, his hands flying around, pulling at his hair.

"What do you mean? Like LEAVING leaving?"

"Yeah, man. I gotta go. I've been here too long. It's time to move on."

"But… but dude, we've… We got it sweet here. We got a cool apartment and we're gonna rebuild the ramp and you're over Trish and Rex is probably gonna not be such a dick and…"

I held up my hand.

"Jase, it's not like I'm breaking up with you."

"When are you coming back?"

"I don't know."

"Where are you going?"

"I don't know."

"This is bullshit! When are you going? I gotta find a new roommate!"

"You already got one."

We both sat down, me on my couch, he on his throne. He pulled his fingers down his face, pulling the sweat in long streaks.

"You're not even gonna ask me to come with you?"

"Oh, come on, we both know your lazy ass ain't goin' anywhere."

He laughed, shaking his head.

"We do have a sweet deal here. But I gotta go. I'm not sure what exactly it is I'm doing, but I gotta go do something. And Rex's sick joke aside, I actually do have a cousin, and she lives in Cali. I might fly out there and check that scene out. I mean, I work online. It's not like I'm in any financial trouble. Hell, maybe I'll try to get in on the porn, instead of just being backstage of the websites."

"Pfft, yeah, good luck with that. No offense, Scott, but Rex is better suited to—"

"Look, either way, I need to meet people I don't know, who don't know me. Chase new girls and skate new spots. I wore this place out, and it was a wild ride, but I need a new game."

"Wait, what about all your stuff? You got tons of awesome shit here! Your room is a vintage tomb of memorabilia and priceless—"

"I'll take what I need and leave the rest for you. Nearly thirty years of action figures, posters, shirts, sheets, clothes, and games. I'm entrusting you with all this."

He saluted me.

"What about your eye? Dude, seriously, you're gonna lose it if it gets infected. You sure it's not too late? At least stick around long enough to get it looked at. I think I see pus."

I smiled, looking down at my dirty worn out shoes but looking up with my eyes to try that trick to stop you from crying. "Yeah, I'm sure it's not too late. I figure I'll hit up the ER tonight and when I'm all fixed up I'll just catch a cab down to JFK and wait for the next flight to Cali. Or maybe I'll go to an ER when I get there. It's a short flight. I can be there tomorrow."

"Tomorrow? Tomorrow! You're really not thinking this through. Did you even call your cousin yet?"

"Nope."

Jase rubbed his face.

"But I did change the password to my savings account, reset the whole profile, and made a substantial transfer from me and Rex's shared bank balance. That's just between you and me."

Jase couldn't fight the smile. Gave me a fist bump.

"Aight, that's rad, but still, this is all so sudden. This is… this is weirder than that night you were on the couch and then you walked in the front door too. It's weirder than last night!"

I leaned back and smiled.

"You're serious, aren't you?" he asked.

"Yeah, Jase. I'm serious."

I got up and walked to the stairs.

"I think you really did hit your head last night."

"Apparently I got shot in it. I need to finish packing."

An hour later, and I was good to go. I had my backpack. Inside was my laptop, some photographs, a couple pairs of socks and underwear, a few shirts, and a football. Wallet and cell phone in my pockets, skateboard under my arm. I stood on the sidewalk in front of our apartment. The sun was bright and high.

Jase sat on the garbage bin in the little gated entrance to our brownstone. I kicked at the gates, staring down the steps leading to our cellar tomb living room.

"You know I ain't gonna hug you or cry," he said.

"I know."

"Bro… good luck, man. I'm gonna…"

I handed Jase my keys. He stared at them hanging there, shining.

"Keep the keys, bro. Rex already has a pair."

"Don't let Rex get to you."

"I can handle him. This is nuts, Scott. You're just BAM! Taking off and leaving everything behind."

"Yeah. It's... exciting. I feel like I hit the pause button by accident and now it's time to play the next level."

"Man, this isn't how it's supposed to end. This has always been a two-player game! Dude," Jase said. He stomped his foot, then looked down. "Why are there hundreds of condoms out here? Magnums? What the hell—"

"Well, how is it supposed to end?"

"You know! You fight your shadow double. And you did that! Then when he's almost beat he flashes red, and then... then you fight the last boss and THEN it's game over."

"The last boss. Who's that?"

"Rex?"

"So Rex is my evil shadow clone mini-boss AND the last boss?"

He spit and grabbed his hair again. "Whatever, that's not the point. You're not supposed to just quit and leave the other player!"

"Leave you? Jase, you ain't losing a friend. You just made a new one. I'd say a shittier one, but no one's perfect, eh?" I slapped him on the shoulder. "Just keep him in line, if you can. Use his laptop to stay in touch or just call me or something."

I slapped my skateboard onto the sidewalk. Started rolling it back and forth with one foot. Adjusted my backpack. I looked down the street toward the BQE, the bodega just barely visible through the tunnel. I aimed my skateboard the other way.

"What am I gonna tell Rex and Trish?"

"Whatever you want. I got my phone working again. You guys can call whenever."

"Argh! This isn't how it's supposed to end!"

"Jase, nothing's ending, trust me. If I'm supposed to come back, I'll be back."

"Yeah, you assume you'd just be let in." He bit his lip. "One more smoke?"

"Sure."

We lit up, yes, smoking pot out on the street in broad daylight. Fuck it.

Not a word was spoken. We stomped the joint roaches out amidst the giant condoms. I looked at my friend, my blood brother, and knew that if I didn't leave right then I never would.

"Aight. I'll call you when I end up somewhere," I said. I smacked Jase on the shoulder. Then I pushed off, felt the thump of the sidewalk beneath my skateboard. I could feel him staring at my back as I slowly rolled away. I held my hand up, giving him a peace sign. "Later, Jase!"

"Later."

I didn't look back.

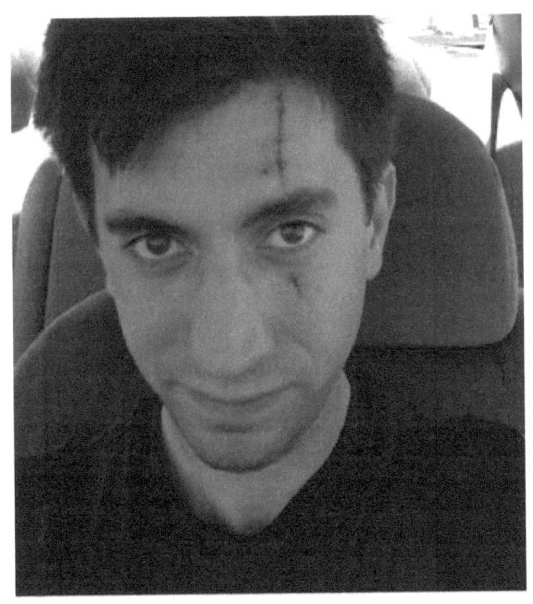

VICTOR GIANNINI is a 29-year-old author and artist hiding out near Montauk, NY. Holding an MFA in Creative Writing and Literature from Stony Brook Southampton, he currently teaches grades 7-12 in the Young American Writers Program.

Giannini's been publishing since 1998 but most recently in the anthologies *Silverthought: Ignition*, *Satirica*, and *Thank You, Death Robot*, and literary journals and magazines including *The Southampton Review*, *Carrier Pigeon: Volumes 1 through 7*, *Other Mag*, *400 Words*, *Italics Mine*, *The Literary Bone*, a lot of weird underground shit, and the legendary *Space & Time Magazine*. This nut also writes and draws a graphic novel, *Skeightfast Dyephun*, designs skateboards, lives for martial arts... and teaches tightrope walking, trapeze, unicycling, and knife juggling. He worships cats, sand, the moon, and claims to have seen a unicorn cry.

Most importantly, Giannini's fiction strives to entertain but also give readers a story where "evil is intelligible, justice is desired, sorrow can be endured, and love remains possible." Actually, one of his mentors coined that literary mission... so Victor stole the concept and ran. Fast. Very, very, fast.

Victor's spirit animal is a fire-fox.

www.ingramcontent.com/pod-product-compliance
Lightning Source LLC
Chambersburg PA
CBHW020142150626
46552CB00021B/1294